the
Gifted

the Gifted

TERRI BLACKSTOCK

WestBow
PRESS

A Division of Thomas Nelson Publishers
Since 1798

www.thomasnelson.com

Published by WestBow Press, a Thomas Nelson, Inc., company, P.O. Box 141000, Nashville, Tennessee 37214 in association with the literary agency of Alive Communications, Inc., 7680 Goddard Street, Suite 200, Colorado Springs, CO 80920.

WestBow Press books may be purchased in bulk for educational, business, fundraising, or sales promotional use. For information, please e-mail SpecialMarkets@ThomasNelson.com.

Library of Congress Cataloging-in-Publication Data

Blackstock, Terri, 1957–
    The gifted / Terri Blackstock.
      p. cm.
    ISBN 1-5955-4061-X (repak)
    ISBN 0-8499-4341-8
    I. Title.
    PS3552.I.34285 G54 2002
    813'.43—dc21   2002069104

Printed in the United States of America

05 06 07 08 09 QW 5 4 3 2 1

OTHER BOOKS BY TERRI BLACKSTOCK

Web page: www.terriblackstock.com

This book is lovingly dedicated to the Nazarene.

INTRODUCTION

Years ago, when I was a divorced mother of two little girls looking for a church home, I went from church to church, desperately seeking a place where I felt accepted rather than shunned—a place where I could grow in Christ and get my life back on track. Thankfully, the Lord led me to that place, and that was the beginning of my healing . . . and my journey back to God.

Some time later, as my pastor spoke to the congregation about our mission to help hurting people, he said that Christians too often shoot their wounded. He said that our church's mission was "to send an ambulance instead of a firing squad." And that's just what that church did for me, through people who'd experienced what I was suffering, and others who used their God-given gifts to minister to me in my time of need.

But I don't see that working in every church, nor do I

see it working in my own all the time. Too often, I see five percent of the congregation doing a hundred percent of the work. The other ninety-five percent just wants to be fed. They sit in their pews Sunday after Sunday, like the man-eating plant in "Little Shop of Horrors" crying, "Feed Me, Seymour!" And the workers do everything they can to accommodate.

That's why I wanted to write *The Gifted*. I wanted to show what could happen if we each used our gifts as God intended. What might that look like in the church? And how would it change us to see God working through those gifts, using every part of the Body of Christ, to minister to a hurting world?

It's my prayer that this book will make readers think about the ways they've been gifted, and prompt them to ask themselves how God might have intended to use those special, unique gifts. Sometimes that gifting takes the form of a talent or skilled service, which God honed in them for a specific purpose. Sometimes it takes the form of an affliction, or an experience of tragedy or suffering, which can be used to help others stuck in the depths of despair. Sometimes it's service or compassion . . . gifts we think aren't important. But God knows they are, and He had a plan for them when He gave them to us.

As you read this book, keep your own gifts in mind. When you're finished, allow the study questions at the end to help you prayerfully seek God's will in your life.

Then imagine the Body of Christ with no paralyzed members, actively laboring in the fields that are ripe for harvest!

1

T HIS JUST ISN'T WORKING." BREE HARRIS CLOSED her Bible and looked at her co-workers across the table. Andy Hendrix and Carl Dennis looked as frustrated as she. "I thought you said this Bible study was going to be an outreach, that we were going to talk it up and get half the office studying with us every Thursday. That was the plan, wasn't it?"

"I thought *you* said you were going to be the one to print out the fliers, telling people about it." Carl Dennis looked disgusted as he got up and crossed the employees' lounge. The office coffeepot was filled to capacity, even though there were only three of them here. "Where are those brochures?" he asked as he poured himself a cup. "I never saw them."

"I was busy, okay? I didn't have time. You could have done them, you know."

Andy sat slumped at the table, his Bible open in front of him. "Bree, you're supposed to be the big desktop-publishing whiz. When we talked about this at church, you said it would be easy. You were even excited about it."

"I know." Bree groaned out the words. "I blew it, okay? I should have done it, but I didn't."

"It's okay." Andy left his Bible on the table and joined Carl at the coffee. "We don't have to have a bunch of people in this. We can do it with just us."

The two men made an amusing picture standing side by side. Andy was six feet four and three hundred pounds; Carl was only five-five and probably weighed 130 pounds soaking wet. But their personalities didn't match their statures. Carl said whatever came to his mind—good or bad—as if he didn't realize that almost anyone in the office could pin him to the floor in the time it took to call him a jerk. Though Andy looked a lot like one of those cocky television wrestlers who ranted and raved threats, he was mild mannered and quiet.

"I know we can do it with just us," Bree said, "but having the Bible study was supposed to be for a purpose. A way to share Christ with our coworkers. I just don't get it. Half the people up here claim to be Christians, but when we start a once-a-week Bible study for thirty stinking minutes after work, nobody has time for it. It kind of makes me mad, you know? I mean, what are the unbelievers supposed to think?"

"Like I said," Carl piped in, "they're not going to think *anything* because they weren't even aware we were having it."

Bree bristled. "Hey, I did put it in last week's newsletter. I also sent an e-mail around to everybody."

Carl sipped his coffee. "Nobody reads those things. I get a million e-mails a day. I delete half of them."

"I also invited a lot of people personally. That should have carried more weight than anything else."

"I did too." Carl sat back down. "I told everybody I've seen for the last three days, and I heard excuses that would singe your hair."

"Well, *we're* here." Andy came back to the table and set his coffee down. "We can do this. I've been working on my lesson all week."

To Bree, that was the biggest problem. When the idea had come up to start this Bible study where they worked, Andy had quickly volunteered to teach it. In her opinion, he was the worst choice. His soft, level monotone would probably put them right to sleep. It was clear that he was following their pastor's admonition to step out of his comfort zone, but she wished they didn't all have to pay for his growth.

She just didn't have the heart to say so. "Okay, Andy. You've got the floor."

Carl came and sat down, but the look on his face said that his thoughts mirrored Bree's.

Andy cleared his throat twice, sipped his coffee, then pulled his notes out of his Bible. "Maybe we could open with a prayer?"

Bree glanced at Carl. "All right."

Andy took both of their hands and bowed his head.

A rumbling sounded over the building, and the coffee in Carl's cup began to slosh. The framed "Character First" sign hanging on the wall crashed to the floor.

Andy's grip on their hands tightened slightly. "It's just a tremor."

But it was more than a tremor. Other pictures fell, and the chairs they sat in began to vibrate and move beneath them. The coffeepot jerked its way across the counter and crashed onto the floor.

Carl jumped up. "Earthquake! Get into a doorway!"

"Not a doorway," Bree cried. "We'll never make it. Get under the table!"

The three of them dove under the table as the

rumbling grew louder. The floor began to crumble, and Bree had the terrifying sensation of hunkering over unsupported plaster that was falling apart beneath her. She screamed.

Plaster from the ceiling began to snow down on them. "The ceiling!" she cried. "We have to get out."

She tried to crawl toward the door, but Andy pulled her back. "The wall's coming down! Cover yourself!"

She got back under the table and covered her head as the wall collapsed on itself, making the rest of the room slant and splinter like a house made of toothpicks. The floor beneath them tilted to one side, rumbling like waves, and the table started to slide.

Bree shrieked out her horror as she began to slide down the incline of the floor. The three-story building above them came down in slow motion, walls crashing, the ceiling caving, people yelling above them.

The light blacked out, and all went dark, but the rumbling didn't stop. The building continued falling on top of them, burying them alive.

2

WHEN THE RUMBLING AND CRUMBLING STOPPED, Bree forced herself to think beyond the panic gripping her. Her body felt bruised, but she didn't think anything was broken. She tried to force her arms through the plaster and concrete pinning her to the rubble beneath her.

"Andy? Carl? Where are you?"

"I'm here." It was Carl's voice.

Relief flooded through her. "Andy?"

Andy spoke up. "I'm here, but I can't move. Something's crushing me."

"Me too," Carl said. "I'm pinned down. Man, three floors fell on top of us. How are we still alive?"

"I don't know." Bree wondered how deeply they were buried. "Maybe we'd better not try to move too much. We might start another avalanche."

They lay silent for a moment, listening for the sounds that might foretell another tremor.

"It was a bad one," Bree said finally.

Andy agreed. "Had to be eight or nine on the Richter scale. We're probably not the only building in town that's fallen."

Bree didn't want to hear that. She pictured the whole town devastated—bridges collapsed, streets buckled, homes and schools destroyed. She thought of her children. Her mother had picked them up from school. They were at home with her by now. Had they been buried too?

Rescue workers were probably combing the streets, looking for victims even now. What if there were so many that it took them days to work their way here?

Horror caught in her throat as she pictured her children buried just like this, unable to help themselves. She imagined seven-year-old Amy's terrified screams and eight-year-old Brad's desperate attempts to dig his way out. *Please God, save my kids!* "Thank goodness it happened after work," Carl said. "There probably weren't many people left in the building."

Andy moaned. "Man, I wasn't even supposed to *be* here today."

Bree tried to concentrate on the sound of his voice. If she could keep her mind focused somewhere else, she might be able to hold the panic at bay. "Where were you supposed to be?"

"I had a doctor's appointment. I was supposed to get a physical, but then I remembered that I was teaching the Bible study so I postponed it. Pretty weird, huh?"

The rumbling started again, and Bree groped for something to hold on to. She screamed as the rubble beneath her shifted and rolled. She felt a hand . . . and grabbed onto it.

"I've got you," Carl shouted. "Andy, grab my hand! Grab it, Andy!"

A cruel roar sounded around them, and Bree heard things collapsing, crashing, falling . . . She felt the impact as debris caved down onto the table pinning them down. She twisted her head sideways and felt as if her neck would pop or her jaw would collapse as the table legs had done. The concrete block wall next to them crumbled and buried their legs. They all screamed out.

Bree began to pray as loud and as hard as she could, pleading with God to spare her, her children, and Andy and Carl.

Then the floor fell out from under her again, and she heard a small explosion and the sound of shattering glass. It sprayed into her eyes, tiny shards of metal and glass, cutting into her corneas and the skin of her face.

It was as though someone had taken an ice pick and made a sieve out of her eyes. She screamed out, but couldn't even get her hands to her face.

Darkness fell over her, and she knew she'd been blinded. If she survived this earthquake at all, she would likely never see again.

Carl fell with the floor, praying that he would hit bottom soon and that the weight of the building would shift and avoid crushing them. Something jagged broke his fall, but his back buckled in pain. He wiggled to move off of whatever lay beneath him, but a steel beam crashed across his legs, pinning him.

Pain shot through him like an internal fireworks display, racking his nerves and stretching his tendons, cracking his vertebrae and crushing his legs.

His screams echoed through his own head, reverberated through the devastated room, and competed with the sounds of the screams he heard next to him.

At first all was dark, then Andy saw the flicker of bright orange dancing through the mounds of rubble that lay next to him. He tried to move toward it, figuring that light must provide some means of escape. But then he felt its heat.

"Something's burning!" He fought to move away, but couldn't. "Fire!"

"We're gonna die!" Bree's cry sounded as though she was still close by.

Carl moaned. "Where's the fire? I don't smell anything."

"It's where I am." Andy choked on the smoke as it filled his air hole. He coughed and tried to turn his head, but he couldn't move. "Help!"

Hot, searing smoke whispered around him to the background song of the crackling fire. He tried not to breathe, but he could only hold his breath so long. Finally, he gasped in air, and scalding smoke shot down his throat, blistering everything in its path, searing his vocal cords, and trapping itself in his lungs.

He coughed and sputtered, but it felt as if the flames were licking his throat, taunting him, destroying him in some slow, evil way. He tried to speak, but his throat felt bloody and ruined.

"Andy, are you all right?" Carl's voice wavered on the edge of panic. "Where's the fire?"

He coughed again, trying to force the smoke out of his lungs, but there was more behind it, growing hotter and more deadly.

"Andy!" Carl's voice was strained and tight. "Andy, move toward me. I'm not getting the smoke. There's clear air toward me."

Andy tried to squirm toward Carl's voice. With all his strength, he managed to turn his body away from the flames and dug through the pieces of concrete next to him.

"I can't move my legs," Carl said. "They're crushed. But I can move my arms. I'll try to dig through to you."

Andy heard scraping next to him, and he tried to match it. Behind him, the rubble shifted again. He dug with his hands toward the sound of Carl's voice until finally he reached the steel beam holding Carl in place. He touched Carl's belt.

Carl's hand grabbed his, and clung for dear life.

"You're okay, Andy. Just get in here where you can breathe."

Behind him, Andy heard more debris moving, falling . . .

The heat of the fire cooled at his back. Maybe the fire had been smothered. He snaked his way through the

12

rubble until he finally gasped a breath of fresh air. "I'm here." His voice was a pitiful squeal. "Fire's out."

"Thank you, God." Carl's hand trembled. "Bree, where are you?"

"To your left, Carl." Her voice was a high squeal. "But I can't see. Glass or metal or something shattered into my eyes."

Andy winced. It was hard to know whose injury was more severe. His throat still felt as if he'd swallowed hot coals, and from the size of the beam across Carl's legs, he was sure that Carl's legs were crushed. And now Bree's blindness . . .

"Try to reach toward me," Carl said. "Grab my hand."

Andy heard scraping again, shifting rubble, grunting . . .

"I've got you!" Carl's voice broke. "We're all together now. We're okay. Let's not let each other go. We'll get through this together."

Bree began to cry, deep, panicked sobs. "My children . . ."

"Let's pray," Carl said. "Come on, Bree. Calm down, and let's pray."

Bree grew quiet, and Carl began to lift up their pain

and fear and panic to the only One who knew for sure what their future held.

When they finished praying through the anguish of their pain and terror, they lay clutching each other's hands, waiting.

"I don't even have a will prepared." Bree hated the eerie way her voice echoed in the silence. "I don't know who will take care of my children. They're so young. They need me."

"We can't give up." Carl's voice rose in pitch, as if he spoke through soul-splitting pain. "We have to get out of here."

Bree tried to push up with her body, but it was no use. "There must be something we can do. Make noise or something. Maybe they're out there looking for us."

"Maybe she's got a point." Carl's trembling hand tightened on Bree's. "Maybe we need to make some noise, keep talking so that if they have any of those ultrasensitive microphones they'll pick us up. We could sing."

"Sing?" Bree couldn't stand the thought. "Are you out of your mind?"

"A hymn," he said. "The Bible says we should praise God in all things. If we need to make noise, singing would do it."

"I know we're supposed to praise Him," Bree said, "but I think He understands if we don't feel like singing now."

"Fine. Then talk, and keep talking until someone finds us."

The pain in Bree's eyes distracted her, and she couldn't think of what to say. So she talked about that. "My eyes feel like a dozen ice picks are stabbing through them. Even if we live, I may never see again—" Her voice broke, and she felt that panic rising again. She drew a deep, calming breath and forced herself to go on. "I don't want to be blind. I want to see my children's faces again. I want another chance to appreciate how beautiful they are. I never appreciate anything! Rainbows, sunsets, snow-peaked mountains . . . I've taken them all for granted. And people . . . I go around looking right through them, never really seeing them . . ."

She let her voice trail off, then finally whispered, "Go ahead and sing. My rambling isn't doing us any good."

Carl cleared his throat. She had heard him sing in church, and he was basically as tone deaf as they come. But that didn't matter now.

He began to sing the chorus to "We Are Standing on Holy Ground," and when he came to the part about angels standing all around, Bree cut in.

"Do you think there are? Angels, I mean."

"If God ever uses angels, and we know He does, I'll bet He's using them now."

Carl kept singing, and finally Bree joined in. The simple song got her mind off of the pain in her caked, bloody eyes, and calmed her panicked spirit.

———

Carl formed the groans in his throat into the words of the song, trying to concentrate on the angels of God hovering around them rather than the angel of death that surely loomed over them. But the pain twisted through his body, making him want to scream.

Wasn't that a good sign? Pain might mean that he wasn't paralyzed. If his spinal cord was damaged, wouldn't he be numb?

He sang on, trying to think of the pain as a good thing, but he couldn't escape the picture of himself in a wheelchair, never able to walk again.

Then he thought of all those nights he'd spent propped up in his recliner watching football on ESPN. Nights he could have been out pounding the pavement to tell people about Christ.

If he was to meet God soon, what would He say about

that? *Wasted a lot of time, didn't you, son? I gave you two per-fectly good legs. Why you kept them propped up all the time as though you were recovering from surgery is beyond Me.*

Carl's response would probably be as lame as the earth-quake had left him. "I worked hard all day, Lord. I thought it would be okay if I just chilled for a while."

He closed his eyes against the regret. *God, please, give me a chance to clean up my heart, even if I can never use my legs again.* He wasn't ready to face the throne of God just yet. There were too many things he had to do—if he ever got out of this place.

He kept singing, forcing himself to be as loud as the pain was intense, praying that someone above all the rubble would hear.

Andy wanted to join in, but his vocal chords felt as if they had melted in the searing smoke. He couldn't make a sound come from his throat.

Even if a miracle occurred and they did survive this live burial, would he ever be able to speak again? He closed his eyes, mentally singing with his friends, trying to make the soft, sweet tune calm him and dull his pain.

What if his vocal chords were ruined, and he could

never utter a word again? What if he never got the chance to say all those things he'd put off saying? There were so many people out there he'd meant to tell about Christ, but he'd hardly ever opened his mouth to tell of his Savior—

He grimaced. What was he thinking? It was probably too late. He probably wouldn't live to tell anyone anything.

When Bree and Carl reached the end of the song, Bree spoke first. "I've always wondered what people feel like when they know they're going to die and leave their children behind. How they manage to trust God to take care of them."

"He will, you know." Carl's voice held a note of determination. "He'll take care of them."

"But they can't go live with their dad. He's not fit to take care of them, and my mother's not capable of doing it alone. She doesn't have much money, and her health isn't good. My sister's got a career. It would just disrupt her lifestyle too much to have two kids in the house."

Andy could hear the despair in her voice. For the first time in a long time, he was glad he didn't have a wife or kids to leave behind.

Bree went on. "I shouldn't have spoiled them so. I shouldn't have spent so much time with them, because now it'll hurt them so for me to be gone. I shouldn't have read them stories at night before they went to bed, or snuggled them up in their beds, or laid down with them until they went to sleep."

"How can you *say* that?" Carl choked the words out. "Bree, those are good things. You shouldn't regret those."

"But I should have prepared them."

"How do you prepare a child for something like this? You can't. You just do the best you can while you're there." Tears filled Andy's eyes at Bree's plight, and for Carl's . . . and for his.

They sang again, one song after another, and Andy locked in on the words assuring him of God's mighty sovereignty, of His goodness and mercy, of His presence in times of distress.

Finally, they prayed again.

"Lord—" Bree's voice was so low that Andy almost couldn't hear—"Lord, if You'll get me out of here, I'll do better, I promise. I won't take so much for granted, and I'll use my time better. I'll devote my life to serving You. Please, won't You give me another chance?"

Silence passed, and they waited. Andy wondered why

they heard nothing above them. No sirens, no digging, no voices calling out.

"At least we all know we're going to heaven if we die." Carl's voice wavered with each word. "We don't have to be afraid."

Andy heard the sound of Bree sobbing. "I'm not afraid for me," she said. "I'm afraid for my kids. I know I'm supposed to trust. I know that whatever God has in store for them, it's right and it's good. And I know He'll take care of them if He takes me out of this life. I even know that maybe He needs for them to go through this to become the people He wants them to be." Her voice broke off. More crying. He wished he could reach her and comfort her in some way.

"I've said that to other people who were dying," Bree went on. "I've written it in condolence cards. And I believe it now . . . but I can't help thinking it would be so much better if it didn't have to happen.

"I'm sorry, Lord." Bree spoke as if He lay there among them, holding her hand with the others. "I know we're supposed to be excited about seeing You. Coming home is supposed to be such a joyful event. It's just that I always pictured it being different, like at the end of my life . . . when I could look back and know that I'd done everything I was supposed to do. I can't do that right now."

Andy squeezed his eyes shut, echoing her prayer. *Me too Lord. I'm sorry too.* Carl started to sing again. Bree began to sing along.

Something shifted, and powder blew down on Andy's face. He squeezed Carl's hand, shutting him up.

"Shhh," Carl told Bree. "I hear something."

Bree got quiet and listened.

Something moved above them. "Do you think it's starting again?" Bree asked. "Another aftershock?"

"No," Carl said. "It's somebody digging! We've got to yell. Everybody yell. Help! Help us! Can you hear us?"

They heard a voice then, and Bree started laughing, a pained, hysterical, gushing relief kind of laughter.

"We're coming for you," the voice called. "Just hold tight."

Andy had heard accounts of near-death experiences, where the dead had seen a white light at the end of a dark tunnel, beckoning them toward the afterlife. When light broke through the darkness of the destruction around him, he knew it meant life for him too. He felt the brisk, fresh air blowing through the hole . . . and his lungs rebelled in a fit of coughing.

"How many of you are down there?"

"Three," Carl yelled up, then the digging got louder and more urgent, and Andy felt the weight of the concrete being lifted off of him, felt steel and bricks falling away.

"We got 'em!" somebody shouted.

Andy heard them working near Bree, scraping and yelling and pulling . . . and finally he heard her voice lifting over his head as they pulled her into the light.

"See about her eyes!" one of the rescuers yelled to the others.

"Get the others out," Andy heard Bree say. "Andy had smoke inhalation and can't breathe or talk. And Carl is crushed. Please get them out!"

He saw them coming back into the tunnel and heard power tools start up. When the buzzing died, someone yelled, "We've got to get Carl first before we can get to Andy. Are both of you all right?"

Carl spoke up. "Andy can't answer. He breathed in a lot of smoke. He's having trouble breathing. He wants you to hurry."

Andy smiled. *Carl, you read my mind.*

It took a few minutes for them to cut Carl out of his vise, but when they got him on the gurney, Andy knew he was going to have to let go of his hand.

He dreaded letting go. Panic sweated over him as he opened his fingers and felt his friend slipping away. What if they got Carl out and the rubble shifted again, this time crushing him? What if the tunnel they'd dug closed up and they couldn't get him out?

His heart hammered out its impatience as he waited for them to come back for him. Then he saw them hurrying back into the hole, and they reached him and pulled him out. It was like sliding through a birth canal, into the light of life. As he came into the day, he felt the jolt of that rebirth, into a world that seemed to have gone haywire.

3

PARAMEDICS SCURRIED AROUND BREE, CHECKING her eyes and sticking a needle into her arm. She could hear rescue workers yelling, television reporters doing live coverage, bystanders chattering and crying.

But she couldn't make out light or shapes, shadows or grays. All was black.

Still, that wasn't the main thing on her mind. "My children! I need to call—"

"Ma'am, we've got to get you to the hospital as soon as possible."

"But if I could just use a cell phone—"

"All the lines are jammed since the quake."

It must have been bad. Horrible. There were probably people buried all over the city. Brad . . . Amy . . .

They loaded her into the ambulance and closed the doors, shutting out the noise. *I'm alive*. She ran that thought through her mind again and again, focusing on the gratitude she felt rather than the paralyzing fear for her children, her mother, her eyes . . .

They reached the hospital in no time, and she jumped as the ambulance doors burst open. Her gurney was jerked out, and she had the strange sense of falling as they raced with her gurney toward some unseen target.

She heard crying and wailing around her, doctors calling out orders, nurses talking loudly to other patients.

"Glass and metal fragments in the eyes," someone beside her yelled. "Vitals are stable. She was just pulled out of the rubble at General American."

Fingers touched her face, probed her eyes. Pain shot through her as they pried her eyelids apart . . . but she still only saw darkness.

Sirens approached, and she heard the rumble of an engine growing near. And then she had the sense of abandonment, as if everyone surrounding her had moved on to someone else.

"Is anybody there?" She reached around her, groping at the air. "Please . . . I can't see."

"In a minute, honey," a woman yelled. "We're helping the more critical patients first."

She thought of Carl, with his crushed legs, maybe even a broken back, and Andy, with seared lungs.

And others around her, in even worse shape.

Bree knew that time was important if her vision was to be saved, but how could she demand attention when people around her were dying?

She lay there, praying in a loud whisper, begging the Lord to take her blindness away. "If You do, Lord, I promise I'll devote my life to serving You."

But the prayer felt limp and lifeless on her lips, for her faith was weak, and she feared that the Lord had plans to use her blindness.

She thought of Paul on the road to Damascus. He'd been living for himself, and for some made-up God he thought he knew, when the Lord struck him blind. He'd been blind for three days, long enough to realize that the Lord was dealing with him. When his sight was restored, he was never the same again. Was the Lord dealing with her too? Would her sight be restored, or would the time ticking by make it more and more impossible for her to be healed?

Bree stopped the direction of her thoughts and decided to be grateful instead. She had been buried alive, and God had sent someone to rescue her. He knew of her plight.

The truth was that she didn't have an ounce of control over anything that happened. Her eyes, and her family, were in God's hands.

4

CHAOS REIGNED AT THE HOSPITAL AND AMBULANCES bottlenecked in the emergency room drive. Doctors stood in the driveway treating patients as they came out of the ambulances, performing emergency triage, rating the patients according to the severity of their conditions.

Carl moaned as they pulled him out of the rescue unit and surrounded him, evaluating his injuries. "Broken bones in both legs, possible vertebral fractures. Immobilize him and give him something for pain."

"Doctor, can't we get him into X-ray?"

"Yes, but he'll have to wait in line. Life-or-death first."

He started to protest, but the group around him dispersed. Then a nurse ran back with a syringe. She fed it into the IV they had inserted in the ambulance. Would he be paralyzed for the rest of his life? Or would his remaining days be plagued with chronic pain? He thought of

Jacob, who'd wrestled with God and wound up with a dislocated hip. The Lord had used that in Jacob's life, and had later made a nation out of that stubborn man. Was this affliction supposed to bring about some change in Carl's life? Was he supposed to accept whatever his condition meant and expect God to work around it?

He didn't want to accept it, any more than he wanted to work around it. *You saved my life, Lord. Please save my legs.*

In moments, relief from his pain seeped over him, and the day grew blurry as he fell into a shallow sleep.

They gave Andy oxygen on the way to the hospital, but breathing came with great difficulty. Once there, they did some respiratory tests and inserted a tube from his nose into his lungs. Then they left him there trying to breathe.

He lay still, slightly panicked, feeling the assault of abandonment. If only someone would come back!

Had they been able to help Bree yet? Was Carl in surgery? Or were they, like him, relegated to the end of the triage line, waiting their turns for treatment?

At least he had a room, unlike those lying on gurneys

all over the parking lot and in the halls. He'd probably gotten special attention because they considered breathing a life-or-death event and they needed to attach him to this machine.

Still, he felt as lonely as he'd ever felt in his life. Even if he could speak, there was no one to speak to.

He thought of his voice, seared and broken. Would his vocal cords ever be restored, or had he been condemned to silence for the rest of his life? They had worked hard keeping him breathing, but no one had looked at his vocal cords to see what was wrong. What if they waited too long to address that?

He thought of another man who had been struck mute—Zacharias, in the Bible. He'd questioned God one too many times, and in answer had been struck dumb until his son, John the Baptist, was born. Andy had questioned God many times. Was he being punished for that now? Would there be an end to this trial, as there had been for Zacharias? If so, when?

A team of nurses and orderlies rolled another man into the room with him, distracting him from his thoughts. The man was unconscious and lay helpless and silent. Another patient was brought in, this one awake but groaning in pain.

Loneliness gave way to a sense of inadequacy. He longed to help these people whose needs weren't being met, but he couldn't think of a thing he could do for them . . . except pray.

5

B REE HEARD HER NAME CALLED THROUGH THE
crowd of injured, and she tried to sit up.

"Bree, thank God you're all right!" Her mother's voice
reached her before she did, and Bree groped toward it in
her darkness.

"Mommy!"

It was her children's voices. She moaned with shiver-
ing relief, and in seconds they were at her gurney, their
arms around her.

She clung to them. "You're all right!"

Her mother touched her face with careful hands.
"Honey, your eyes . . ."

"I'm blind, Mom. I can't see. And they're so busy with
the others . . ."

Her seven-year-old, Amy, began to wail, and Bree

pulled her close again. She wished she could see her face. "What's the matter, honey?"

"I'm scared. Look at your face, Mommy!"

She heard her son sniffing, and she reached out for him too. "You're not crying, are you, Brad? Mommy's okay."

"Your eyes! They need to fix them."

"They will, honey. Real soon."

It sounded as though Bree's mother was crying too. "What can I do for you, sweetie? I want to help you, but I don't know—"

"You can take the children home." Bree kept her voice calm and steady. "Now that we each know the other is all right, you should take them home and let the doctors deal with me here. The kids don't need to see me like this. It's upsetting them."

Her mother pushed her hair back from her face. "But we don't want to leave you."

"It's a madhouse here, Mom. There are too many people. They'll get to me soon. Just go home and pray."

When her mother finally kissed her good-bye and took the children away despite their cries to stay with her, Bree fell back onto her pillow, exhausted but grateful. The Lord had answered two of her prayers: she'd been rescued, and her children were fine. She prayed that someone would come and tend to her wounds soon so that she could go home to her children and hold them as they fell asleep tonight.

Later that night, a doctor made it into her room. He stood beside her bed with his hand on her shoulder, and she wished she could see him. "We're doing surgery on your eyes in the morning," he said, "but there's significant damage."

His weary voice didn't sound hopeful. "Will I see again?" she managed to ask.

There was a long pause. "We'll do the best we can, Ms. Harris."

"What does that mean?"

He sighed. "Nerves have been damaged, and the cornea was lacerated. I'll try to get the glass and metal out and repair as much as I can, but I can't promise that your sight will return."

After he left, Bree lay in the silent darkness that cloaked her. She was too numb to think, too numb even to pray. Finally the pain medication worked through her system, and Bree fell into a dreadful, shallow sleep.

6

THE NEXT MORNING, BREE FELT THE LIGHT OF DAY through the window, warming her face. Slowly, she opened her eyes.

She saw light! She turned her face to the window, where she saw clouds floating through the sky, a tree just beyond the glass. And around her, she saw the other injured patients.

"I can see." She sprang off of her gurney and looked around for a nurse or doctor. "I can *see!*"

Had they done surgery on her last night when she'd been asleep? Wouldn't she have awakened for part of it? Wouldn't she have bandages?

She saw a bathroom, ran into it, and looked into the mirror. The cuts on her face and eyes were gone, and she looked as unharmed as she had yesterday before the quake. How could that be? No surgery could have healed her cuts that quickly, restored her vision, and erased her scars.

She came back out of the bathroom, and a nurse rushed toward her. "You should have called me, honey. I would have helped you."

"I can see! Look at me."

The woman clapped her hands over her own face and stared at Bree. "How can that be?"

"I don't know."

"But they didn't do surgery yet. They didn't do anything!"

Her heart hammered with realization. She had been healed, not by doctors or equipment or cleverly mixed drugs.

God had healed her.

"I'm going to get the doctor!" The nurse raced out the door.

Bree went back to her gurney, looking around for someone else to tell.

On the gurney next to her lay a high-school boy, blood caked on his disfigured face. Clearly frightened and traumatized, he looked up at her and met her eyes.

Flash.

The boy was no longer a teen, but a child, kneeling in a dark attic, screaming and banging at the door to get out.

"Daddy, please let me out. I'll be good. I promise I'll be good."
He had a black eye, and his face was pale as if he hadn't seen
the sun in days.

Flash.

Bree blinked, then stared at the boy, who was once
again a teen, once again stretched out in front of her on
the gurney. What in the world had just happened? Here
she stood, in a busy hospital room, staring at a boy who
had just been through an earthquake, yet she'd seen a little
boy in an attic . . . and she knew it was him.

Had it been a vision of some kind?

She was shaking, she realized, and she turned her eyes
from the boy. "I need to go home."

Her heart pounded as she tried to get away from the
boy whose past she had just glimpsed, and she walked
through the gurneys toward the door.

The nurse bustled back in. "Ma'am, the doctor will be
here soon. You need to lie down until he comes."

Flash.

It was nighttime. She saw the nurse tending to her sick
husband. He was ill and could hardly move for himself.
Vomit stained the sheets, and the woman moved around like
a zombie, exhausted by her work schedule by day and her
caring schedule by night.

"It's okay, honey," she whispered as she stood over her

husband. "I'll clean it up." She worked the sheet out from under him, cleaned his face and his neck, changed his shirt, then managed to change his sheets out from under him.

Exhaustion and dejection painted her features as she lay down beside him and slid her arms around him. "You're going to be okay, honey. I'm here."

But he wasn't there, not really, and loneliness radiated from the woman's broken heart.

Flash.

The nurse reached for her to move her back into bed.

Bree started to run, dodging the gurneys, zigzagging through the people, until she finally got out into the sunlight and took off running, running, running, until she came to a convenience store where she went in and asked for a phone.

Desperately glad to be out of that place, she called her mother to come and pick her up.

7

CARL WOKE ON THE SAME GURNEY HE'D BEEN brought in on, still strapped down . . . but the pain was gone. He wiggled his fingers and managed to get one hand free, then felt his legs. They seemed straight and whole.

Wanting to see for himself, he managed to pull the brace off of his neck and slowly sat up and looked down at himself. His pants were still torn, but the blood was gone, and the legs that he'd seen last night—all mangled and bent like pieces of wire twisted in all directions— looked perfectly normal.

Slowly he peeled back the straps holding him to the bed and pulled his legs free. They moved without pain or trouble.

"I can't believe this," he whispered. "How in the world?"

He moved his legs so they hung off of the gurney, then slowly slid his feet down until they bore his weight. He stood on them, expecting searing pain to shoot through them, but there was no pain at all! His legs felt stronger than they'd ever felt before, and an urgent need to move filled him.

"I can walk." He marched across the floor, then jumped and spun around. "I'm healed!"

He knew without a doubt that the Lord had shown him mercy. No doctor had done this. It was clearly an act of God.

He wanted to tell someone, but that urgency to go rose up inside him, drawing him barefoot out of the room. His feet ran and skipped around the gurneys that blocked the hall.

Those feet led him faster, faster than his mind could keep up. They led him between gurneys and around the corner, up the hall. And then they stopped beside the bed of a boy who lay sleeping.

Carl looked down at the child and saw that his lips were blue. His skin looked as gray as death itself.

The boy wasn't breathing.

Carl grabbed his shoulders and shook him. The boy remained limp. "Help!" He yelled at the top of his lungs as he scanned the hallway for a nurse. "This boy isn't breath-ing. Somebody help!"

A nurse came running, saw the boy's condition, and called out a Code Blue. Doctors and nurses from all over the floor raced toward them to revive the child.

Carl stood back, watching as adrenaline shot through him, twisting around his confusion. How had he known to walk right up to that boy? It was as if his feet had known the child's condition.

How could that be?

He looked down at his bare feet. They looked the same, but something was different. That urge to walk had overcome him again.

He gave into it, and suddenly his feet were making that mad dash again, though he had no idea where they were taking him.

He left the hospital and went out into the bright morn-ing. He started walking in a direction away from his own home, and then picked up his speed until he ran one block, and then another, turned a corner, and went down a hill.

He saw a team of people digging at a collapsed build-ing, still trying to rescue anyone who was buried.

His feet led him to another collapsed building across the street, but no one was digging here. Instead, a crowd of people stood out on the street talking and chattering, as if grateful they had survived the quake.

Carl turned, staring at the rubble. His skin crawled with a certainty so powerful it nearly knocked him down. Someone was in there, trapped in the collapsed building. He grabbed a man on the sidewalk. "Is everyone in this building accounted for?"

The man nodded. "Yes. I work there. I'm pretty sure everyone got out."

Carl knew that wasn't true, though he couldn't have said how he knew. He took off running around to the back of the building where the wall had caved in. The man followed, staring as Carl stepped over the rubble. "How do you get to the basement?"

"Well, there's a stairwell—" he pointed—"but you shouldn't go in there. The building's probably unsound."

Despite the warning, Carl bolted toward the stairwell. He reached it and threw the door open. He started down the stairs . . . then stopped cold.

It was as if the ground had just come up in a heap to swallow up the floor and walls of the basement. There was nothing but dirt and rubble on the side where the building's wall had caved in.

There were people down there. He knew it with absolute certainty.

He ran back up. "Get some workers over here! There are people in there!"

Several of the firemen from across the street came running over and down the stairwell to see the rubble.

"Get some equipment over here!" one of the firemen shouted. "They could be alive."

"They are!" Carl's voice trembled with urgency. "I can tell you right now that they're still alive."

He didn't know how in the world he knew such a thing, but he had no time to question it. He had to get to those people before it was too late. He grabbed a shovel and started digging with the firefighters, determined to rescue these people who had somehow drawn him to their aid.

Within an hour, they made contact with the people who were buried, and one by one they managed to get them out, all alive. One man couldn't feel his legs. Another had a severe head injury and was unconscious. Two came out almost unscathed. When the fourth man came out, Carl knew they were finished. There were no others.

He turned and raced up the street, running like a track star for a couple of blocks, though his lungs panted and gasped for breath. A crowd of people stood in front of a store that sold televisions, and they watched the monitors as the news covered the earthquake damage.

He stopped in that crowd, looking around. He had expected to find another building, more people buried, rescue workers with shovels, but instead there were just people standing and looking at the television monitors, tears on their faces.

He saw a man in the crowd and quickly walked toward him. His feet seemed to know that the man needed help, but Carl stood there not knowing what to say or do. The man gave him an uneasy look.

"May I help you?"

"No . . . uh . . . I'm sorry."

Something strange was happening to him. He felt the man's pain, as if there was something within him that needed rescuing, but Carl didn't have a clue what it was.

He suddenly felt very tired. His head had begun to ache, and he thought about his parents in North Dakota. They had probably been calling his house all night, frantic to know if he was alive.

He needed to get home. He needed to make contact with the important people in his life. He needed to rest.

A tidal wave of weariness and confusion crashed over him, crushing him with its weight until he could barely stand. Trembling, he started walking home.

8

A NDY DIDN'T REALIZE HE'D BEEN HEALED UNTIL his sister and her husband showed up at the hospital that morning. He still had a tube down his throat, but it didn't burn like it had yesterday, and his breathing came easier.

When the doctor made rounds, he pulled the tube out, and it was only then that Andy knew something had happened.

"I couldn't talk at all last night," he said in a rapid-fire cadence. "I'm telling you, I couldn't talk. My throat was burned, and my lungs felt parched, and I had blisters in my mouth and down my trachea. And now there's not a trace of smoke inhalation, not a cough or a wheeze or phlegm in my throat or anything. Do you think I've been healed?"

The doctor looked baffled and went to study his test results again.

Andy looked up at his sister, Karen. "I thought I was a dead man yesterday, and I was in a lot of ways, but I'm telling you something strange happened to me last night. I shouldn't be able to talk at all." He glanced at the man on the bed next to him, who was watching and listening quietly. "Sir, I'm telling you that I was healed miraculously, just like in the Bible. It's almost like Jesus came in and touched me and I was healed, only I don't know why He'd heal *me*, of all people, because I've never been much of a soldier in His kingdom. It's not like I'm worthy of a miraculous healing, but I'm telling you that's what's happened."

Karen started to laugh. "Andy, I don't think I've heard you say that many words in a day, much less in a minute!"

"I know!" Andy swung back around to her. "But all of a sudden I feel like I just have so much to say. I have to tell everybody about the miraculous healing power of a God who cares about us. Jesus is good! I don't know how it happened, but I know *what* happened, and God healed me just as surely as I'm standing here with you."

The doctor came back in, still reading his chart and scratching his head. "I can't explain it. When we looked at your vocal cords and your lungs last night, you were in serious trouble."

"I'm well now!" Andy lifted his hands to the ceiling. "Examine me and you'll see."

The doctor listened to Andy's lungs and looked into his throat. Finally he pulled the stethoscope from his ears and gave Andy a long look. "You can go home, I guess. You look fine to me."

Andy sprang off of the bed, hugged his sister, and slapped his brother-in-law's hand. "I'm outta here."

Karen just stared up at him. "You're not acting like yourself, Andy. Are you sure you didn't hit your head?"

"I was only buried under a three-story building, Karen. I hit my head and everything else. But nothing on me is hurt."

"But you're not acting like yourself."

"I don't know what you mean." He started out into the hall, not even bothering to wait for the paperwork that would release him. When he came through the door, he bumped into a gurney parked there. A woman lay on it, groaning.

He stopped and bent over her. "Ma'am, I'd like to pray for you if you don't mind. See, I was healed, and the Lord who owns the universe and everything in it has the power to heal you too. So I'd like to pray and ask Him to send you the help you need, to comfort and help with your pain."

The woman started to cry. "Get away from me."

A nurse touched his shoulder. "Sir, can I help you?"

"I just wanted to pray for her," he said. "I didn't mean to upset her, but she's obviously in pain, and I thought prayer might be something that would help her because it sure helped me. I didn't mean to offend her."

"She'd rather be left alone," the nurse said calmly. "If you don't mind."

Andy gave a plaintive nod. "Sorry."

He walked to the next gurney and bent over it. "Sir, do you know the Lord? Because I do, and amazingly and miraculously, He healed me this morning after I'd inhaled smoke while buried under a three-story building. And I feel that I have to use my voice now to glorify and praise Him, and what better way to do that than to tell everyone I see about the love of Christ—"

Someone grabbed him and pulled him away from the man. He turned to find it was Karen. She glanced from side to side, as if he'd embarrassed her. "Andy, you've got to stop talking. They're going to call security."

"But there are people who need to hear what happened to me, and I can't stop speaking about what I have seen and heard. I think that's a verse from Acts 4, when Peter and John were arrested and told not to speak anymore about Jesus, and they said they couldn't stop speaking about what they'd seen and heard. I know exactly how they felt now, because as much as I'd like to, I can't seem to stop talking about it."

He pulled away from her then and stopped a nurse coming his way. "Ma'am, do you understand how precious you are in God's sight? Do you know that He knit you in your mother's womb, and that He knew you even before the foundation of the earth was laid?"

"Well . . . uh . . ."

Karen's husband, Ed, grabbed Andy's arm and pulled him away. "Come on, bro. They're going to admit you in the psychiatric ward if you don't shut up right now."

Andy towered over his brother-in-law, but he allowed him to pull him from the building. "You've never told me to shut up in your life, Ed. What's gotten into you?"

"I've never *had* to tell you to shut up! You don't talk much. It's not your nature. You're quiet and pensive and mutter a lot."

Karen grabbed his other arm. "Andy, I know you're excited about being healed, but it wouldn't hurt to rest your vocal cords to keep from straining them again."

"I'm fine." They went down the front steps of the hospital and toward the parking lot. "I'm just realizing that when the Lord gives you a gift, you have to use it for His glory, and I've been given a gift. I've never thought of my voice as being a gift from God, but it is, Karen, and yours and Ed's are too. Only I've had something so amazing happen that I can't help feeling marked by God in some way, like He has a special plan for these vocal cords of mine, and if I'm quiet about it I'll just be throwing that gift back in His face, and besides, I don't think I could hush if I wanted to, because I just have all these words right on the tip of my tongue, and if I don't let them roll off, I think I might wind up in that psych ward, after all."

They got into his sister's car, and he ducked his massive frame into the backseat. "So where were you guys when the quake happened?"

"We were both at home, thankfully," Ed said. "It didn't do too much damage in our part of town."

"Well, what if that had been different?" Andy leaned up on the seat. "What if you had been in a building that collapsed? Say you died. Do you think you would have gone to heaven?"

"I don't know if I believe in an afterlife," Ed muttered.

"What if you're wrong?"

Ed rolled his eyes. "Andy, I can't deal with these hypotheticals right now, okay? I'm just going to take you home."

Andy wasn't daunted. "I'm serious, Ed. You need to think about that, you know. Everybody needs to think about it, especially in light of what just happened. I mean, if you don't believe in an afterlife, you must have reasons for it. But one of us is wrong, and I think it's you."

Ed chuckled. "Well, you're entitled to your beliefs, and I'm entitled to mine."

"We're going to find out someday, Ed. I mean, I survived this, but I'm going to die one day, and so are you."

"Not for a while, I hope."

"Could be today . . . or tomorrow. There could be another quake in the next few minutes, and the ground could swallow us up, and we could all be lying there dead."

Karen's mouth fell open, and she gave him a disgusted look. "Andy!"

"You can't hold off death forever," he went on. "That's my point. There's going to come a time when you're going to find out for sure whether there's a heaven or a hell. Now, while you can, you need to consider Jesus Christ, like it says in Hebrews 3:1. The Bible also says that broad is the way that leads to destruction. That the way to heaven is through a narrow door, and that door is Jesus Christ."

Ed just stared straight ahead as he navigated his way across town. "Whatever you say, Andy."

"I just challenge you to consider it, okay? It's not God's will that any should perish."

Ed pulled the car into Andy's driveway. His small house looked unharmed. He hadn't even considered the possibility that it could have been damaged in the quake.

"Where's your car, Andy?" Karen's effort to change the subject was apparent.

"I guess it was crushed in the quake. I'm not sure. The insurance will probably take care of it soon. Good thing we live in a small town. I can walk just about anywhere I need to go."

"Call us if you need a ride anywhere."

He nodded, but didn't make a move to get out. "Will you both think about what I said? I could get you a Bible if you need it. I have a couple of extra ones."

"No thanks." Ed was more than annoyed.

Andy got out of the car and closed the door, then started to lean in the window to continue the conversation. Ed started pulling out before he could do that.

Andy waved helplessly. "I don't know why you won't listen to me." He knew they couldn't hear, but he felt compelled to say it. "I'm just trying to tell you the greatest news in the world."

Slowly he walked into the house, dropped his keys on

the table, and stared at the phone. He had to call someone. He still had a lot of talking to do. He sat down with
his phone and the telephone book and started through his
list of friends.

He hoped they would listen.

9

THE BROTHERHOOD COMMUNITY CHURCH HAD suffered its own damage in the earthquake. The roof on the northeast corner of the building had caved in. While most of the building still stood, the damage was extensive enough that the leadership feared having the congregation meet in there for the Friday-evening service. Instead, they congregated in the fellowship hall to pray for those still buried in the rubble, for the rescue workers and medical personnel caring for the injured, and for all those grief-stricken people searching for their loved ones tonight.

Bree arrived at the church with her mother and her children and greeted one of the deacons who stood at the door.

Flash.

She saw him as a younger man, walking through a jungle wearing combat fatigues, a gun slung from his shoulder. His face was painted in camouflage. His comrades walked in front of and beside him, listening, their guns poised to shoot.

The sound of machine-gun fire startled them all. The young man next to him hit the ground . . . then another . . . and another, until he was left standing alone.

A bullet ripped through his leg, and he fell, too, still firing at some invisible target.

Flash.

"Bree!" The deacon was speaking to her with a huge smile. "I heard you'd been injured in the crash. I didn't expect to see you."

Shaken by the vision, she swallowed hard. "Uh . . . James, are you a veteran, by any chance?"

His face changed, and that smile faded. "Well, yes. I fought in Vietnam."

Then the visions were true. She felt a little dizzy and reached out to steady herself.

"Why do you ask?"

"I just . . . heard it somewhere. Come on, kids . . ."

She took her children's hands and escorted them past him. Tears came into her eyes, but she knew that if she started crying, she might not be able to stop. Something was wrong with her. Maybe it was a head injury. Maybe she did need to be back in the hospital.

Quickly, she took a seat at the back of the room.

Across the room she saw Carl coming in—and she stared. He looked perfectly healthy! The legs that she was sure would be paralyzed strode into the room. Carl didn't even have a scratch on his face. She watched him walk the perimeter of the room, as if he was too fidgety to sit down.

Then she saw Andy filing in with a group of people. He was deep in conversation, and she wasn't able to catch his eye. His voice seemed to be working now.

The service began, and she tried to concentrate on praying. But the moment the service was over, she turned to her mother. "Mom, can you take the kids home? I need to talk to Carl and Andy."

"Sure. Do you want me to put them to bed?"

"No, they can stay up. I'll tuck them in when I get home."

Her mother and children scurried off, and Bree crossed the room to Carl. She hugged him. "Carl, I'm so glad you're okay."

"You too, Bree. Man, I didn't think so when I saw you after they pulled you out. How in the world can you look so good? Your face was cut all over and scraped and bloody, and your eyes were swollen shut."

"And you . . . how are you walking?"

59

Carl shook his head. "It's the weirdest thing."

"Man, I've got to talk to you two." They both turned and saw Andy towering over them. "Do you have a minute? Something weird has been happening."

Bree frowned. "What do you mean, something weird? Andy, how are you talking?"

"I've been healed—"

"Me too!" Carl said. "Man, I woke up this morning as good as new, like yesterday hadn't even happened."

Bree brought her hand to her face. "And you can see by my eyes that the same thing happened to me!"

"But it's more than that." Andy looked from side to side, keeping his voice low. "Can we go somewhere private and talk?"

Bree hesitated. Something weird, Andy said . . . Had he and Carl been seeing visions too? "Yeah. Let's find a Sunday-school room." She led them out of the fellowship hall and into the hallway.

But Carl wasn't following her lead. He'd turned to go the other way, into a group of people clustered near the exit. She tried to catch up with him, and Andy followed behind her. Carl stopped next to a woman who stood off by herself, listening to the chatter of the group.

When she saw Carl standing beside her, looking as if

he was waiting for something, she got an uncomfortable look on her face. "Can I help you?"

He just stood there. "Uh . . . no."

Then Bree met her eyes.

Flash.

She saw her as a small child, maybe four or five, being dragged, kicking and screaming and crying, from her home and put into a human-services car. Her parents stood at the door cursing and screaming threats at the people who were taking her. She saw the child being belted into the backseat, heard her crying and wailing for her parents as the police snapped handcuffs on them—and dragged them away for drug charges.

Flash.

Bree broke out in a cold sweat as Andy came up behind them.

"Man, there are people out there who need us. We've got to tell them about the Lord," he said. "I mean, we can't expect to just sit in here and have people come to us, you know. I know there were a few new faces in here tonight, but for the most part we've got to go minister to them where they are, because how can they know unless they are told, and how can they be told unless someone is sent, and how can they be sent unless—"

Carl grabbed Andy and headed the other way up the hall. "Come with me."

Andy kept chattering as Carl led them to a room. Bree closed the door and switched on the light.

"Something weird is happening," Andy said again. "I think I'm losing my mind."

"Me too," Carl said. "Don't tell me. You feel like your feet are taking you all over the place, like they know things you don't know, and you can't be still no matter what you do?"

Andy and Bree looked at each other. "That's what's happening to you?" Bree asked.

"Yeah." Carl kept pacing. "Ever since my legs were healed, it's like they have a life of their own. If that's not what you meant, then what's happening to you?"

"I can't shut up," Andy said. "I've been talking people to death. Everybody I see . . . witnessing and quoting Scripture like it's my last day on earth or something. Like I have to cram a lifetime of lost opportunities into one minute."

Bree gaped at them both. "And I see things."

Both men turned to her. "What do you mean?"

"I've been having visions. I mean, really weird visions, like if I look somebody in the eye—not every time, but real often—if I look somebody in the eye I have this flash into his or her life. I see defining moments when something terrible happened. Like that girl outside, Carl, that you were just standing beside. Why did you take us up to her?"

Carl shook his head. "I don't know. It's the weirdest thing. It's like my feet are taking me places I don't want to go, and when I get there I know somebody is in danger, and I feel this urgency. I led some firemen to some people buried under rubble today. How I knew they were there, I don't know. Something supernatural is going on here. I can't stop it, and now I'm walking up to people in crowds and just standing there. I know they need help. I know they're in danger, but I can't seem to figure out what it is I'm supposed to do next. And that girl out there, she was one of them. I just felt like walking up to her, and then I stood there and I didn't know what to do."

"And then I saw a flash into her life," Bree said. "That girl was taken from her parents when she was a tiny little girl. She saw the police arrest her mom and dad on drug charges."

"How do you know that?"

"I told you, it's these visions. I just *saw* it. I've been

63

seeing into people's lives all day. It's just bizarre, and it's making me crazy."

"I know just what you mean." Andy took her shoulders. "I'm chattering my head off and driving people away left and right, but I can't seem to stop it. And the weird thing is I'm quoting Scripture that I didn't know before."

Bree sat down. "You've only been a Christian for, what, a year?"

"Yeah, and I've always had trouble memorizing. Now all of a sudden I'm quoting Scripture like crazy."

Carl frowned. "You don't think we've been given some kind of supernatural gifts, do you? I mean, God spared our lives, but maybe he also had some wild purpose for our survival."

"It doesn't feel like a special gift." Bree hugged herself. "It feels kind of like a curse. I'm scared of it. I'm almost afraid to look into anybody's eyes."

Andy bent down to her. "Well, why aren't you seeing into my past? You're looking in *my* eyes."

Bree shrugged. "I don't know. It doesn't happen with everybody. I saw a lot of people when I came in here tonight, people greeting me and hugging me and telling me how glad they were that I was all right, and I didn't have the flash then. I only had one flash then—it was of

James Miller in Vietnam. But I sat down after that and didn't look up until the service started."

Carl began to pace again. "So I felt an urgency to walk up to that girl, and then you saw a vision into her past."

Andy stared at the floor, as if piecing the puzzle together there. "Yeah, and then I opened my mouth and started rambling, only I didn't know what she needed to hear."

Carl's eyes widened. "Do you think maybe we're supposed to be working together? I mean, I've been running all over town all day. It's been so weird, and I'm exhausted, and I don't feel very productive, except for that time that I showed the firemen where those people were trapped. Maybe if I had Bree to follow up with her visions into people's lives, and you, Andy, to talk to them, it would make some kind of sense."

"I think you're right." Andy's eyes rounded. "Maybe we're supposed to work together to fill people's spiritual needs and help them see that Christ is the answer. That's the reason we're here, isn't it, to continue the work that Jesus started? Ephesians 2:10 says that we are His workmanship, created in Christ Jesus for good works, which God prepared beforehand, that we should walk in them. And what are those good works supposed to be? Well, of *course* we're supposed to tell people about Christ. I mean, that's our main job as Christians, isn't it?"

Bree stared at the air. "You know, I've only shared Christ with two people in my entire life, and I've been a Christian for fifteen years. Those two people are my children."

"Well, that's nothing to sneeze at," Carl said.

"It's nothing to brag about either. I mean, I've always known I was supposed to bear fruit as a Christian, but I kind of adopted the attitude that people would know by my actions. I just haven't been very proactive. Why in the world would God have chosen me to have a gift like this? Why would He trust me with something like that?"

"I don't know," Carl said. "I don't know why He would choose me, either. I mean, look at me, the short, skinny bald guy, all of a sudden running all over town like an Olympic athlete. You'd think I'd bust an artery or something. I haven't gotten this much exercise in years."

"And me," Andy said. "Quiet Andy. Too cool for conversation most of the time, and here I am, just overflowing with Scripture and wisdom that I don't have."

"Okay, so let's go over this again." Carl walked to the front of the room and used his hands to sort it all out. "I know where to go, and Bree, you know what the problem is because you can see into people's lives. And Andy, once you know the problem, you know what to say."

Andy started to laugh. "Maybe I'm not crazy. Maybe we're all just anointed."

"Anointed?" Bree repeated. "Oh, boy. I'm scared. I'm not a very daring person."

"Well, all you have to do is see," Carl said. "I'll take you to the person; you see the need. Tell Andy what it is, and he'll do the rest. I say we go out right now and test it."

10

CARL, YOU'RE GOING TO HAVE TO SLOW DOWN!"
Bree struggled to keep up with his quick step as he
led them blocks away from the church. Andy jogged along
beside him, dripping in sweat.

"I'll try," he said. "But I feel like we need to hurry."

"Where are we going, anyway?" Bree looked around
them.

"I'm not sure, but my feet know."

Bree laughed. "Do you know how stupid that sounds?"

"Of course I do. It's downright ridiculous, but it happens to be true."

The hospital came into view, and Carl's feet picked
up their pace. "Okay, now I've got it. We're going to the
hospital."

Bree gasped. "Oh, no! I don't want to go back there."

"Here am I. Send me, Lord," Andy muttered. "We

have to make ourselves available, Bree. That's what we do, we Christians. We're obedient; we go where we're told."

"Theoretically." Bree wished she'd worn more comfortable shoes. Her feet were beginning to hurt.

When they got into the hospital, she looked around and saw that every available space was still occupied by a bed. People lay in various states of consciousness, with head injuries, broken arms, mangled legs. *Everyone* here was in danger. Everyone needed help. How would they ever isolate which person they were supposed to talk to?

But Carl seemed to know where he was going.

He led them through the gurneys to an exit door, then trotted up one flight of stairs, Andy and Bree right on his heels. A doctor walked toward them in the corridor, staring down at a chart.

Carl walked straight up to him, blocking his way.

The doctor looked down at him. "Excuse me." He stepped to his left, but Carl stepped to the right, continuing to block him. Then Bree met the man's eyes.

Flash.

She saw him lying in bed, the alarm clock blaring. His hand trembled as he turned it off, then got out of bed and rubbed his face. She watched as he went to the liquor bottle on his dresser, poured some into a glass, and threw it back.

Flash.

She quickly turned to Andy who stood behind her and whispered one word. "Alcoholic."

Andy stepped up to the doctor, and Carl moved aside. Bree saw that the man's hands trembled, just as they had in her vision.

"You need a drink, don't you?"

Bree blinked at Andy's blunt question, and the doctor gave him a startled look. "What did you say?"

"I said you need a drink, don't you? Bad. But maybe not that bad since you've probably already had a couple of swigs today."

The doctor took a step back. "Look, I don't know who you are, but if you don't get out of my way right now, I'm calling security."

"The Lord sent us here to talk to you, Doctor," Andy said, "and I intend to be obedient. You've sold yourself into slavery to alcohol, but I know how to set you free."

The hardness on the doctor's face melted, and he stepped back against the wall. His mouth began to tremble, and slowly, he seemed to crumble apart.

Then Andy started talking.

Not too long into Andy's conversation, Dr. John Fryer led them into a consultation room. A Gideon Bible sat on a table in the corner, and he grabbed it and began looking up Scripture as Andy quoted it.

Before long, he had given his life to Christ.

As Andy and the others rose to let John Fryer get back to work, he touched Andy's arm. "Do you really think God can deliver me from this alcoholism?"

"I know he can." Andy's voice rang with confidence.

"We have some church members who have beaten addictions," Bree said. "I know if you came there we could hook you up with them and they could help you."

"I've been to AA." John rubbed his eyes. "The twelve steps make a lot of sense, but it's always seemed like there was something missing." He pointed to the Bible. "I think this is it."

"It *is* it," Andy said. "I can promise you that. There's deliverance in the Holy Spirit. Come to church with us Sunday, and we'll introduce you to some people who can help you."

John still had tears on his face as he returned to his work.

Carl grinned and gave Andy a high-five. "That was absolutely awesome, man! I've never seen anything like it. Andy, you did a fabulous job."

"Well, you didn't do so bad yourself." Andy grinned.

"And Bree, the way you saw into that guy's life. I mean you nailed him with one word."

"Yeah, but it wouldn't have done any good if you hadn't been there to follow through. And without Carl, I would have been bouncing all over the place looking into people's eyes and having these weird visions that scared me to death."

"We're a team, man. The dream team," Andy said. "I feel so empowered. That man's life will be changed because of today, and who knows how many other people will be affected by that?"

Carl started leading them back to the stairwell, and they both followed behind him. "Carl, are you doing it again?" Bree asked.

"You got it," Carl said. "Man, I'd love to stop and rest on our laurels, but it looks like there's more work to do."

"Lead us on, man," Andy said.

He led them out of the hospital and to an old apartment complex sporting graffiti on the wall. Vagrants loitered on the sidewalk out front.

Bree hesitated. "I'm kind of scared to come to this place. Are you sure this is where we're supposed to be?"

"Absolutely sure." He started up a flight of stairs, and Bree and Andy tried to keep up.

"Don't be scared, Bree," Andy said. "The Lord says, 'When you pass through the waters, I will be with you; and through the rivers, they will not overflow you. When you walk through the fire, you will not be scorched, nor will the flame burn you.' That's from Isaiah 43:2."

Bree considered the Scripture. "In other words, He's with us, so I don't need to fear."

"That's right."

She nodded. "Okay. Then I won't." She tried to catch her breath. "How many flights, Carl?"

"I don't know. I'll let you know when we get there." He went up two flights, then came around to the walk in front of the doors. He stopped at the third one.

"You're just going to knock on the door?" Bree asked.

"Yeah, and when they answer, you do your bit."

"I have no control over this," she said. "If it happens, it happens."

Carl banged on the door. They heard footsteps across the floor, and then the door cracked open.

"Yes?" A woman with a black eye and busted lip peered through the crack to them. Bree met her eyes.

Flash.

She saw her being beaten up by her husband, kicked and

knocked with his fist until she was down on the floor, screaming for mercy.

Flash.

"Can I help you?" Fear shone in the woman's black eyes.

Bree stepped forward, trying to be brave. "Uh, ma'am, I know this sounds really weird, but the Lord sent us here because your husband beat you up."

The woman opened the door further. "How did you know that?"

"I told you."

"Don't give me that 'Lord' bit." She peered out past them. "Did the police send you here?"

"Police?" Bree shook her head. "No. Why would they?"

"Because they arrested my husband." She started to cry and stepped back from the door.

Andy stepped inside. "Ma'am, can we come in? We really need to talk to you."

"Fine, come on in."

They came into her dilapidated apartment and looked around. The furniture looked like it had come from someone's garage sale, but only after being abused for forty years. A broken lamp sat in the corner.

The woman sat down, her movements careful, as if less visible parts of her body were broken and injured too. "Now tell me the truth. Why are you here?"

"Ma'am, it's true what we said about the Lord leading us. He cares about you."

She pulled a cigarette from a pack on the table and grabbed a lighter. "If He cares about me so much, then why doesn't He just let me die?"

"He must not be ready for you to die," Andy said. "We're here to tell you how you can live."

"How I can live?" She took a drag of the cigarette and blew it out slowly. "A better question is *where* I can live since my husband got hauled off to jail for beating the stew out of me. I don't have the money to pay my rent that's due on the first of the month. That gives me about five days to find another place to live." She tapped the ashes of her cigarette into an empty beer can. "Oh, and did I mention that I don't have a job?"

"What's your name, ma'am?"

"Sarah Manning."

Andy made formal introductions of the three of them, then quoted the Scripture about how God provides for the birds of the air and the flowers of the field, and then he told her about the ultimate provision God had made for her.

After a while the woman's angry, defeated tears turned to tears of wonder. Her heart seemed to soften, and she began to hang on Andy's every word.

Finally, she agreed to meet them at church on Sunday.

As they started to leave, she came to the door with them. "I think you were right. God really did send you here to me tonight. I wish you had come in time to save my husband too."

"It's not too late for your husband," Andy said. "We have people at our church who do prison ministry. Maybe we can send someone to help him."

The woman dabbed at her eyes. "Looks like God is into miracles these days. Who knows? Maybe He has one for him."

As they left the old apartment complex, Andy and Carl slapped hands again.

"That was just as cool as the first one," Carl said. His step was slower than it had been earlier. "But you know we have to help her. Besides her spiritual needs, she needs a place to live, a job, and money."

"Yeah." Bree looked back at the woman's door. "Makes you wonder, doesn't it?"

"Wonder what?" Andy asked.

"Well, if God gave us these gifts, it makes you wonder

if He didn't give others gifts that would follow these up? Maybe we just haven't found them yet."

"Could be," Andy said. "We'll just have to keep our eyes open."

Carl came to a corner and stopped walking. "Man, I'm exhausted. I feel like I've spent the whole day running a marathon. I could just fall on the sidewalk right here and go to sleep."

"I need to get home, anyway." Bree looked at her watch. "I promised to put my kids to bed. I think I just need to lie down with them and cuddle up for a while. Maybe we could start again tomorrow."

"Sounds good to me."

They headed back to the church. A comfortable silence fell over them as they strolled back with no particular urgency. When they got there, they stood looking at each other for a moment.

"What do you think?" Bree looked from Andy to Carl. "Tomorrow's Saturday. Do we get back together and try it again?"

"Sounds good to me." Carl slumped against his rental car. "My feet are going to be taking me places whether you guys are along or not. You might as well come so we can get something done."

Before they separated they prayed for Dr. John Fryer and Sarah Manning, who'd just accepted Christ. They prayed that the Holy Spirit would do His work to comfort them tonight and keep them firmly planted in their new-found salvation.

11

THE NEXT DAY, BREE'S MOTHER OFFERED TO KEEP her kids while she went out "witnessing" with Andy and Carl. It had occurred to Bree that perhaps she should tell her mother about the extraordinary gift she'd been given, but her mother tended to be an alarmist, and Bree didn't want her thinking that her daughter had some kind of brain injury and rush her to the emergency room. She also didn't want her children to absorb any anxiety from their grandmother. So she chose to keep the matter to herself.

She met Andy and Carl in the church parking lot. Carl paced back and forth, raring to go, and Andy chattered nonstop. When Bree got out of her mother's car, Carl yelled out, "Okay, you're here. Let's go. Hurry!"

"Hurry?" Bree locked her purse in the trunk of her car. "Hurry where?"

"I don't know! I'm just ready to go."

She dropped her keys into her pocket. "Okay. Feet . . . take us away."

Carl shot her an unappreciative look and started walking.

"Don't mock him," Andy said. "'He who mocks the poor reproaches his Maker.' Proverbs 17:5."

"Hey, I'm not poor," Carl said, breathing faster as his step picked up. "I probably make the same thing you make."

"Well, I'm poor," Andy said.

"Me too," Bree piped in. "Dirt poor. I'm the one who has to live with her mother."

"'Blessed are the poor in spirit,'" Andy said. "Matthew 5:3."

"We're not talking about poor in spirit." Bree was glad she'd worn her walking shoes today. "I'm talking poor in wallet. And now I've got to get a new car, and the insurance almost never gives you what your car is worth."

"What did we tell Sarah Manning last night?" Andy breathed hard as he kept up with Carl. "That God provides. 'But seek first His kingdom and His righteousness; and all these things shall be added to you.' Matthew 6:33."

Carl turned and took off up a hill.

Bree trotted behind him. "I'm glad this is a small town. Can't your feet press an accelerator instead of pavement, Carl? We could use my mother's car."

"I think I have to walk. But don't worry. We're here." He led them into another older, deteriorating neighborhood and turned up a sidewalk. "Someone inside this house needs us."

Bree thought of Sarah Manning last night, thanking them for coming. She drew in a deep breath for courage. "Okay. Go."

Carl knocked and stepped back, letting Bree have center stage.

But no one answered. Bree tried again.

Finally, they heard a voice from deep in the house. "Help! Somebody, please help!"

Bree shot an alarmed look to Andy and quickly turned the doorknob. It was unlocked, so she pushed the door open. "Hello?"

"In here."

A woman's weak voice came from the kitchen. Carl bolted through the house and led them to an old woman lying on the floor.

"Thank God you've come . . ." Her words were slurred.

Flash.

Bree saw the woman lying on the floor, trying to get up, but one side was paralyzed. She'd had a stroke, and no one was there to help her. Bree watched her turn to her paralyzed side and push up with her good hand until she managed to get to her feet. She took a step and fell again.

"God! Can You see me at all? Are You there? Do You remember me?"

Flash.

"Call an ambulance," Bree said. "She's had a stroke. Ma'am, how long have you been lying here?"

"Since yesterday." The left side of her mouth didn't move with her right as she spoke.

Bree and Andy got the trembling woman up and carried her to the couch while Carl called for the ambulance.

"God sent you." She turned her faded eyes to Bree's face. "I prayed and prayed for help." She reached out a trembling hand. "I'm May Sullivan."

They each introduced themselves.

"Yesterday, when she couldn't get up, she felt like the Lord forgot her," Bree whispered to Andy, who took the baton.

"Ma'am, do you know the Lord?"

"He knows me." May chewed out the words. "Sure seems to, don't He?"

"Yes, ma'am, He does." Andy's words were soft and gentle. "But He doesn't just want you to get medical help. He wants your spirit healed too. Ma'am, the Lord wants me to tell you what it says in Isaiah 49, verses 14 through 16: 'But Zion said, "The LORD has forsaken me, and the Lord has forgotten me." Can a woman forget her nursing child, and have no compassion on the son of her womb? Even these may forget, but I will not forget you. Behold, I have inscribed you on the palms of My hands.'"

Tears began to run down the woman's half-paralyzed face, and Bree heard a siren approaching the street. The woman reached out for Andy's hand. "Come to the hospital with me. I need to hear more of what the Lord is saying to me. I did think He'd forgotten me. But He ain't, has He?"

"No, ma'am. He hasn't forgotten. We'll come with you and finish this conversation."

The paramedics were the same ones who had rushed Bree to the hospital the day before, and because she pleaded with them—and they were so amazed that she had walked out of the hospital without any of the injuries with which they'd taken her in—they broke the rules and allowed all three of them to ride with the woman to the hospital.

Bree and her friends waited with May, and Andy told her of God's love and the fact that He'd never had her out of His sight. When she had been admitted, they promised to come back and visit her later. She hugged them good-bye as if they were family.

As they left the hospital, they ran into Dr. John again. "Hey, guys." He looked better than he had yesterday, and Bree was certain he was sober, though his hands trembled slightly, and his skin had a gray cast. She supposed his body would have to adjust to its new state. "Were you looking for me?"

"No," Bree said. "We just brought a friend in. She had a stroke, and we found her on the floor of her kitchen."

"What's her name?" Dr. John asked.

"May Sullivan. She's in room 413."

"I'll stop by and see her. So . . . about church tomorrow. I was going to call you."

"You're not backing out are you?" Andy asked. "Come on, man, you need to be there."

"I know." He raised his hands in a mock vow. "I'm going. I just wanted to make sure you didn't forget. I hate going in places like that by myself. I haven't been to church since my best friend's wedding. That was six years ago."

"We'll meet you on the front steps," Carl said. "You won't be the only one. There are a few others we'll be meeting too."

"Great." He patted Carl's shoulder. "I'll be there."

Carl was already starting to walk off, and Bree knew he'd been hit again with that foot thing. So she said good-bye to Dr. John and took off following him. Andy was close behind.

They hurried out of the hospital and up the sidewalk, and Bree shook her head. Where in the world would Carl's feet lead them now?

12

C ARL DIDN'T LEAVE THE HOSPITAL CAMPUS. INSTEAD he led them around the building to the courtyard beside a pond, where patients and staff members sat on benches, smoking their cigarettes or staring at the water. Carl's step slowed as he reached a man who sat facing the water, his arms crossed, a stricken, pained look on his face.

"Him?" Bree asked, and Carl nodded.

Bree stepped up to the man. "Excuse me, sir?"

He looked up, and met her eyes.

Flash.

She saw him holding his wife in a dark hospital room, lit only by the night light above her bed. She wept against his chest, and he wept with her. "My baby. Everything was going to be so perfect. One more week, and he would have been born. One lousy earthquake changed everything."

"At least you're all right." The man's voice was pained, strained.

"I wish I was dead," she said. *"I want my baby."*

Flash.

"Do I know you?" The man frowned up at them.

"Uh . . . no." Bree wondered how to proceed. She couldn't very well tell Andy what was wrong right in front of the man. No, she was going to have to start this herself. "I'm so sorry about the death of your baby. How did it happen?"

He shook his head. "The earthquake. My wife fell when our floor caved in. It's a wonder she wasn't killed too."

Bree looked up at Andy.

He took the seat on the other side of the man, then held out his hand. "Hi, sir. My name's Andy Hendrix. Do you mind if I sit down for a minute?"

The man shook Andy's hand. "Sam Jones. No, I guess not."

"I don't know if you've ever read Psalm 116:15, but it says that 'precious in the sight of the LORD is the death of His godly ones.'"

Sam brought his wet eyes to Andy. "It's not so precious to me."

"No, it never is to us, but your baby's in heaven, and you have the opportunity to see her again."

"Him." Sam cleared his throat. "He was my son." He started to weep again and covered his face to hide it from them.

Andy touched his back. "God understands your pain. His Son died too. An excruciating, cruel kind of death."

The man looked up at him, his features twisted. "I know all about the cross. Never made any sense to me. And the bit about God giving up His only son . . . If there *were* a God, why would He do that? Why would He let Him die?"

"He let Him die because that was why He was born," Andy said. "Jesus came for one purpose: to die so we wouldn't have to."

"Then why do we?" Sam challenged. "If He came to die for us, then why isn't my son alive? Why aren't my parents still here? Why do I have to visit them at their graves?"

Bree watched Andy, waiting to see his answer. She wasn't sure she could have answered that herself.

"It all goes back to Genesis," Andy said. "When man fell. He had a perfect world, and then Satan tempted him. Told him he could be like God and that he wouldn't die. But Adam died, and so did Eve, and so has everyone in the world since that time. Jesus came to stop that cycle, to give us a chance to live, to take on Himself the punishment that we've all deserved because we've all sinned. Hebrews 5:8–9 says that, 'Although He was a Son, He learned obedience from the things which He suffered. And having been made perfect, He became to all those who obey Him the source of eternal salvation.'"

"Obey Him in what? What has God ever asked me to do for Him?"

"Obey by believing in Him. If you do that, we're told that we do not grieve as those who have no hope. That when Jesus comes again, the dead shall rise first. Yes, your little son will rise first, and then you'll join him in the clouds. We'll be caught up together with him in the clouds to meet the Lord in the air, and we'll always be with the Lord."

"Jesus is coming again?" Sam shook his head. "I don't even know if I believe He came the first time."

"I'm betting my eternity on it," Andy said. "So are you, whether you do it consciously or not."

The man stood. "I have to go back to my wife. She needs me. I just came out to get some air." He looked at Andy, then Carl and Bree. "I appreciate you talking to me like this, but I'm not much into religion, you know?"

Andy sprang up. "We go to Brotherhood Community Church. Our service is at 11:00 tomorrow morning. If you can, try to come. At least hear the Lord out. He's after you. He sent us to talk to you because He knows the pain you're suffering."

Sam nodded and offered them a weak wave. "Thanks. I'll think about it. My wife's getting out this afternoon, though. I don't think I can leave her that soon."

They watched him as he headed back up to the hospital, his head hung low.

"So much pain," Bree whispered. "I wish you could have helped him. But I guess even a supernatural gift can't do miracles."

"Of course it can," Andy said. "We planted some seeds. I'm sure of it. The Lord led us here as a team, just like He's done with all the others. It wasn't in vain."

"So should we check on him later, or what?"

"Let's just see what God urges us to do." Andy grinned. "He'll let Carl's feet know."

Already, Carl had started walking, and Bree and Andy followed.

13

They saw six more people accept Christ before the day was over, and planted seeds in the hearts of eight others. The next morning, Bree, Andy, and Carl showed up early for church, hoping to talk to their pastor before Sunday school and church began.

They found him in his office, going over his sermon notes. Carl knocked on the door, and the pastor looked up.

"Hey, Jim," Carl said. "Can we talk to you for a minute?"

Jim got to his feet and laughed as he saw the three of them. "Well, sure. Come on in. I always have time for the miracle trio."

"The miracle trio?" Bree shot Carl and Andy a look. "Why do you call us that?"

"Because that's what you are. Pulled out of the rubble after being buried for five hours? And not one of you hurt? It's a miracle, that's all there is to it."

"Oh, yeah," Bree said. "I guess you're right. I thought you meant . . . something else."

"Something else?" He laughed. "Like what?"

Bree sat down, and Carl and Andy took seats on either side of her.

"Well, see, uh . . . it's like this," Carl began.

Andy blurted it out. "We've been given some real strange supernatural gifts, and we've been sharing Christ and seeing lost souls turn to Him all over town."

Jim frowned. "Supernatural gifts? What do you mean?"

Andy looked at the others. "I mean . . . we can do things that we couldn't do before. Soul-winning things. Fruit-bearing things."

"Well, that's great." Jim clapped his hands. "That means you're growing. I could tell last week when you said you were starting a Bible study at your office that you were growing and stretching. I've been so proud of you guys."

"No, that's not the kind of gift he means." Bree shifted in her seat. "Not the plain old ordinary work-of-the-Holy-Spirit kind of gift."

Jim laughed out loud. "The 'plain old ordinary work of the Holy Spirit'? Bree, you've got to be kidding. There's nothing about the work of the Holy Spirit that's ordinary."

"I just mean—"

"She means that we're doing some really bizarre things," Carl said. "I have this walking thing. My feet just start walking, and I find these people who need our help."

"Well, that's good, Carl. That's great. We should all be willing to go where the Lord wants to send us."

Bree wanted to shake him. "But I have this vision thing. I can look in someone's eyes, and I see pain and loneliness and things in their lives that have made them into who they are."

Clearly, Jim loved it. "The Holy Spirit is making you sensitive to other people, Bree. See? There's nothing ordinary about that. Yes, it's supernatural. It sure is."

He wasn't getting it. Bree looked at the others. "But Andy is talking, saying things he never would have said."

"Yeah, man," Andy piped in. "I'm quoting Scripture like crazy and teaching and explaining the gospel like I never could before."

"Because you've been studying your Bible," Jim said. "See, Andy? I told you that the more you knew, the more confidence you would have to talk to others. You've always had a teaching gift. That's why I encouraged you to lead the Bible study at your office."

A knock sounded on the door, and Stanley, the choir director, leaned in the door. "Jim, can I see you for a minute?"

He got up. "Excuse me, guys, I'll be right back."

When he was gone, they sat staring at each other.

"Do you believe that?" Bree asked.

Andy started to laugh. Bree joined in, and Carl followed.

"He doesn't get it. He thinks we're just doing regular Christian things."

"I don't know why," Carl said. "We never did them before."

"Well, maybe this is another God thing," Andy said. "Maybe we're not supposed to tell anyone. Maybe we're just supposed to be obedient and keep it all to ourselves."

Bree got up, went to the doorway, and looked out into the hall. "Do you think so?"

"I don't know," Carl said. "Hardly matters, though, if he isn't hearing what we're saying."

Jim came back in and slipped back into his chair. "Sorry. Sound problems. We're expecting a big crowd today, after the earthquake and all. Now, where were we?"

Andy looked at the others, then drew in a deep breath. "We just wanted to let you know that a bunch of the people who have come to Christ in the past couple of days will be visiting our church this morning."

Jim clapped his hands together again. "Great. What are their names? I'll make sure I meet them."

Bree smiled. "Well, uh . . . there are about a dozen of them, I think."

"No, fifteen, I'm pretty sure," Carl said. "They may not all come."

"Fifteen, if you just count the ones who gave their lives to Christ," Andy said. "But some of the seeds God planted could take a little root. A few of those could come too. Could even be twenty or so."

Jim straightened slowly in his chair. "You guys have talked to twenty people about Christ? What . . . did you speak to a rally this weekend or something?"

"No," Bree said. "We've just used our gifts. The ones we told you about."

Jim stood up. "This is amazing. This is just what I needed to hear. My message today is designed for the seeker and the new believer. I wanted to take the opportunity the earthquake gave us to reach those whose hearts were made tender by the disaster."

Carl began to laugh. "Well, we're bringing them so you can preach to them. Only some of them have some pretty serious problems. There's a doctor who's an alcoholic and a woman whose husband abused her."

"The husband's in jail," Bree added. "And she wants us to talk to him . . . only I don't think they'll let us visit him until he's been there a while."

"There's a man whose wife lost her baby in the quake," Andy said. "And then there's May—"

"May?"

"Yes. May's an old woman we found who'd had a stroke and lay on the floor over twenty-four hours. She's in the hospital. She might watch us from television."

"Okay." Jim paced back and forth. "I think I'm getting the picture now."

Bree sighed in relief. "You are?"

"Yes. We can't just stop with a sermon. We have to set up a kind of spiritual triage. These people are hurting. We have to rely on all of the parts of the Body. We have people who can help with grief, and others who've kicked alcoholism, and we have a group who does prison ministry, and there are dozens in the church who are great at serving . . . taking food and giving rides and checking on the elderly."

Bree looked at Carl. "People with gifts that follow up where ours leave off."

"That's right," Jim said. "We're all gifted differently, for just this kind of thing. Trust the Body, Bree. Let it work. I'm so glad you gave me a heads-up this morning. I'll use the Sunday-school hour to go around and gather up some help. Keep bringing them in, guys, and we'll take care of them here. They won't leave this place without knowing how much the Lord loves them."

"Thanks, Jim. We knew we could count on you."

"No. Thank *you*." He came around the desk and hugged each of them. "One of the things you learn in seminary is that the true test of the effectiveness of your ministry is when you see your fruit bearing fruit. You're doing it, guys. You don't know how much that means to me."

14

B Y THE TIME BREE, CARL, AND ANDY MADE IT TO the front steps where their visitors were to meet them, Sarah Manning was already there. Her eye was still swollen and black, but it was clear that she'd tried her best to hide her injuries with the deft stroke of a make-up brush. She looked awkward and out of place.

Bree hurried toward her. "Hi, Sarah. I'm sorry I wasn't out here sooner. I was talking to the pastor. I hope you had the chance to meet some of our members."

"I sure did." Sarah looked around. "That's the problem. I'm not used to all this. I'm kind of the type that likes to keep to myself, you know? I don't like crowds or a lot of people." She seemed jittery, like she needed a cigarette. "I don't know if this church thing is going to work out for me. I mean, I still want to be a Christian and all, but I just don't know if I can do this crowd stuff every week."

Bree looked around, wondering which of the members had insulted her. "Was someone rude to you?"

"Oh, no, they weren't rude. I got, like, three invitations to lunch, and several invited me to sit with them. And I don't know. I just kind of freaked out. I didn't think I could handle it anymore. I was just about to leave."

Relief and gratitude flooded over her. So none of them had undone her efforts with Sarah. She was just overcome by the love.

"They're just trying to love you," Bree said. "It's what they do at church, at least when church is working well. Don't hold it against them."

"Oh, I don't." Sarah hugged herself. "It just blew my mind. I've never seen anything like that. It's just going to take some getting used to."

"I'll stay with you, but please say you won't leave. God brought you here for a reason. Some day you'll think of these people as family."

Sarah's smile was tentative. "All right, I'll stay."

Bree wanted to hug her, but she feared making her change her mind. Behind Sarah, she saw Carl and Andy with the others who had come, and she recognized the man whose baby had died. A lump of emotion formed in her throat. She hadn't expected to see him again.

"Come over here." She took Sarah's hand and led her toward them. "I have some people I want you to meet."

She could almost feel the woman stiffening beside her as they headed to the group. But as she made the introductions, she felt Sarah relaxing. It was clear that the others were as nervous and uncomfortable as she.

Jim preached the best sermon of his life that morning. Bree sat among the people they'd met in the last couple of days. Sarah sat next to her, riveted on every word the pastor said. Her awkwardness seemed to have melted, and when the altar call came, she got up and went to the front. Bree sat stunned in her seat, amazed by the Holy Spirit's work to make her take such a public stand. Several of the others went, as well.

When the service was over, Bree wiped her tears, then hurried to find Sarah in the back.

Sarah was dabbing at her own eyes, but she had a serene smile on her face.

Bree had to laugh. "That took a lot of courage."

Sarah shook her head. "I think it would have taken more courage to sit there and not go."

"You seem more relaxed now."

"Yeah. Church was different than I thought. I expected people to be judging me, but they weren't, you know? They were nice."

"Listen, why don't you come home with my family and me and eat lunch? I mean, it won't be much. Tuna sandwiches, probably, but the kids and my mother and I would love to have you."

Sarah glanced at the exit door, then brought her big eyes back to Bree. "I don't know. I'm not too good with kids."

As if on cue, Bree's children came running up to her. "Mom, Mom! Can we go home with Danny and his family?"

"Both of you?" she asked.

Danny's age fell between the two of them, so they'd all been close friends since they were in the nursery together.

"Did Danny ask you, or did his parents ask?"

"His parents," her son said. "Mom, please? We never get to do this."

Bree had hoped to go to the hospital to look in on May today. "Well, let me talk to Danny's parents."

Her children ran and got Jeanine, the boy's mother. "Let them come home with us, Bree," Jeanine said. "Heaven knows, you need a break with all that you've been through lately."

"Well, I just feel like I haven't been spending enough time with them."

"Mom, we can have quality time later!" Amy cried. "Come on. Let us go."

Jeanine laughed. "We can keep them all afternoon, then bring them back to church tonight. You can take them home then. It'll be fun. They'll have a good time."

Bree grinned down at her children. "Okay, but give me a kiss." She hugged and kissed both of them, then watched them scurry off.

When they were gone, she turned back to Sarah. "Well, now that I don't need to go home, I think I might just give my mother some quiet time to herself and walk to the hospital to visit a friend. Do you want to come? We could get a bite to eat there. My treat."

Sarah thought that over. "I guess that would be all right."

"Are you sure the crowd at the hospital won't bother you?"

"Oh, yeah, it's not that. It's these people . . . loving me, you know. I'm not used to that."

They started to walk out of the church and headed toward the hospital. Bree studied Sarah. "So you don't mind strangers. You just don't know how to react to people who want to be close to you?"

"Yeah," Sarah said. "I know it's stupid. I probably need

therapy. I *know* I need therapy. It's been a long time since I've had anybody really show me any affection, and today I must have gotten like eighty-nine hugs. Usually when someone comes at me, it's with a fist."

It was a beautiful day, and a breeze whispered through their hair. The sun shone with such serenity that no one would ever know there were things in the world like earthquakes and fires, and people who beat up defenseless women.

"Why would you marry a guy like that?" Bree asked. "I'm just curious. You're a real pretty lady, and you have a sweet spirit. I don't understand why you would bond yourself with somebody like that."

"That's the million-dollar question, and I'd love to have it answered. But here I am, and the truth is, every major relationship I've had has been like this. Men always woo me in the beginning. I start thinking he's just what I've been looking for, the fulfillment of all my dreams, and then I wind up sleeping with him. The next thing I know, my face becomes his favorite punching bag."

"Did you know your husband was abusive before you married him?"

"Yeah, I pretty much did. Kind of felt like I deserved it, you know? Like I did stupid things that caused him to hit me. I thought I could change him. But it never happens that way."

They reached the doors of the hospital and went in, quickly ate a bite, then headed up to May's hospital room.

"You don't have to come in with me," Bree said. "You can wait out here."

"That's okay." Sarah kept walking with her. "I'll come. You said this is a lonely old woman. Wouldn't hurt for me to make friends with somebody as lonely as me. Just as long as you're sure she won't reach out to hug me."

Bree started to laugh. "I'm sure. She's pretty helpless right now."

They got to her room, and May sat up in bed, carefully trying to feed herself with her left hand. But the food kept dribbling out on the stroke side of her mouth.

"How are you today, May?" Bree asked as she came in.

May looked up. "Oh, my rescuer! Come in here, darling. Come in."

Bree came to her side and leaned over to give her a hug. "How are you feeling today?"

"So much better." She looked at Sarah over Bree's shoulder. "And who is this?"

"This is Sarah Manning. She's a new friend, like you."

"Ain't she wonderful?" May asked Sarah, nodding

toward Bree. "You know, she saved my life, she and her two friends. They just showed up at my door when I'd been laying on the floor praying my guts out that somebody would come."

"I heard," Sarah said, "but you look wonderful today."

"I *feel* wonderful. Oh, that Dr. John, he said he knew you and that was why he came by. He's took over my case. He got me the help I need, and he's just a wonderful man."

"Really? John Fryer?"

"Yes. Oh, he's such a giving person . . . so attentive. I've never had a doctor that attentive."

"Wow."

May brought her hand to her heart. "And we talked about the Lord."

"You did?"

"Of course we did. He said that you had helped him turn to Christ, and that his whole life had changed. He told me about the drinking. He's gonna give it up. I know he's gonna kick it."

"Of course he is," Bree said. "But I'm kind of surprised. It just happened yesterday, and already he's reaching out and giving of himself? That's pretty amazing."

"It's a miracle, that's what it is!" May slapped her hand

on the bed. "Another one of God's miracles, just like sending you to me. We've struck up a friendship, Dr. John and me, and I think it's going to last a long time."

She reached out for Sarah's hand and pulled her closer. "Now, tell me about you, dear."

"Well, I guess I'm another one of Bree's converts," Sarah said in a soft voice. "I was like you. I was kind of in my house praying to God for help. My husband had beaten me up, and he was arrested that night, and I realized I was probably not going to have the money to pay my rent, and I wasn't going to have a place to live, and all of a sudden, what do you know? These three people knock on my door and come in and tell me that somebody loves me." Her voice broke, and tears came to her eyes. "I'm sorry," she said, quickly rallying. "I didn't mean to do that."

"Mean to do what?" May asked. "Cry? Well, honey, everybody needs to cry now and then."

"I know, but not in front of strangers."

"Well, I'm not a stranger," May said. "I'm your sister in Christ. Don't you know that?"

Sarah smiled and dabbed at her eyes.

"Now what's this about you not having a place to live?"

Bree jumped in. "Her husband was arrested after he beat her up. She can't afford to pay the rent."

Sarah nodded. "It's due tomorrow, and I don't have the money. It's a dump, anyway. Landlord has already found new tenants, so I have to move out. I'm sure I'll find some place to go. I'll probably go to a women's shelter until I can find a job."

May's face lit up. "Well, why don't you stay in my house?"

Bree caught her breath. "May, are you sure?"

"Of course I'm sure. There's my house, sitting there all empty. As long as I'm in the hospital, I need somebody to look after it." She turned back to Sarah. "You might as well sleep there. I have a guest room, so you can even stay when I get home, and maybe you can give me a hand now and then."

Sarah slowly sat down on the chair next to the bed. "Do you mean that?"

"Of course I mean it. You'd be helping me. I can't go home alone. I'll have to learn to walk again, and it's not gonna be easy. Sarah, do you drive?"

"Yes ma'am," Sarah said, "but I don't have a car. It got repossessed a couple of weeks ago."

"Well, maybe you could drive mine and get me to

physical therapy every day. I mean, until you get a job." May caught her breath as another thought occurred to her. "On second thought, *I* could give you a job. You can be my personal helper until I can get on my feet! What do you think of that?"

Sarah's eyes filled with tears as she looked from May to Bree, and back again. "I think that's the most amazing thing I've ever heard in my life. Talk about answered prayers."

"Prayer works," Bree whispered. She had tears in her own eyes as she leaned over and hugged May. "You don't know what this has meant to me."

"To you?" May asked. "I wouldn't even be here if it weren't for you. It means life to me."

"Abundant life." Bree's throat constricted, and she swallowed hard. "We told you, didn't we?"

Sarah laughed softly. "Man, you sure did."

They heard footsteps running up the hall, then Carl squeaked around the doorway, his tennis shoes almost skidding across the floor.

"Bree, I thought I'd find you here." He was so out of breath he could hardly speak. "I have to go. I have to go *now.*"

Bree turned back to Sarah and May. "I need to go with him. I think there's somebody else who needs us."

"Sure. Go," May said. "You do what you gotta do."

"Yeah," Sarah said. "I'll just stay here and get to know May a little bit better."

Bree grinned as she followed Carl out the door. Andy was just coming off of the stairwell when they walked out into the hall.

"Man, you're getting faster," he said to Carl. Carl was already heading back down the stairs.

"You guys won't believe what just happened," Bree said as she ran down the stairs. "I brought Sarah here to have lunch, and then we went up to see May, and the next thing I know, May's telling me how Dr. John Fryer has been ministering to her and taking care of her."

"Really?" Andy mopped the sweat off of his face with his sleeve.

"Yeah, but get this: Sarah's sitting there telling May that she doesn't have a place to live, and the next thing you know, May is inviting her to come live with her! Then Sarah mentions that she doesn't have a job, and May hires her to be her assistant when she gets home."

Carl looked back over his shoulder. "No way. Are you kidding me?"

"I'm not kidding. This is all working out, just like Jim said. Our fruit is bearing fruit. Can you imagine?"

"Did you see what happened at church today?" Carl turned a corner. "I've never seen anything like that in my life. Every one of the people we brought got ministered to. Some of them even went home with church members. I noticed that Dr. John went home with Greg Browning."

Bree gasped. She knew that Greg Browning had almost drunk himself to death years ago, but he hadn't had a drink in over seven years. "That's great! He's just the one I wanted to introduce Dr. John to."

Carl nodded. "If anybody can help John, it's him."

"That's nothing," Andy said. "I saw Sam Jones—the man whose wife lost their baby—going home with Dennis Simmons and his wife. They lost their baby last year."

"Oh, that's perfect!" Bree punched at the air. "The Simmonses will be able to help so much with that family."

"I think so." Carl breathed as hard as Bree and Andy, but his feet seemed to move faster and faster.

"Carl, can you slow down just a little?"

"I don't think so," Carl said, so Bree broke into a trot. She should have changed her shoes after church, she thought. Carl finally took them into a pretty, middle-class neighborhood with well-groomed lawns and houses that were only a year or two old. Bree frowned. From her lower middle-class home with her mother, she had often wondered if people who lived in houses like these really ever had any problems. And yet, here they were, beating the pavement, a holy task force headed to rescue another soul. They rounded a corner, and a house came into view with cars parked along the street and filling the driveway. People came and went with covered dishes in their hands.

"Looks like somebody is having a party," Andy said.

Carl turned up the sidewalk. "That's where we're going. Right there. That's the house."

"No." Bree grabbed him by the shirt and tried to stop him. "Carl, we can't go in there. Look at them. They're having a party. How would we know which person needs us?"

"I don't know, but this is where God is telling me to go. And trust me. It's very urgent."

Bree groaned and looked at Andy.

"We might as well follow him," Andy said. "He hasn't led us wrong yet."

So they trudged up the sidewalk toward the front door. And just as they reached the front steps, a woman came out. She was wearing a black dress and had tears on her face.

Bree stopped. "Hello."

The woman covered her mouth. "It's terrible, isn't it? A real tragedy." Then she headed out to her car.

Looking back at the woman, Carl stopped at the front door, his chest heaving. "Did you see anything when you looked at her, Bree?"

"No," Bree said, "but I'm getting a feeling that maybe this isn't a party, after all."

"Funeral." Andy watched the woman's car drive away. "It's a funeral."

"How do you know?"

"Well, look what everybody's wearing." He nodded to a group who had come out the side door. "Mostly black."

Bree saw it now. "Oh, they sure are. You think it's for someone who died in the earthquake?"

"Maybe," Carl said. "It could be ours, if God hadn't rescued us."

Bree's throat constricted. She thought of her mother grieving, her children clutched together, mourning over their lost mother.

Why had she been spared, and someone in this house had not? She forced herself to step up to the door, but Carl stopped her.

"Wait. I thought this was it, but it isn't."

"Oh, thank goodness. I didn't know what to say—"

"I mean, it's the house all right, but not inside." He led them down the porch steps and started around the back of the brick house.

"Carl, where are you going? You can't just walk into people's backyards. We're trespassing." But Carl wasn't listening. Reluctantly, Bree followed him around the house. Andy came too.

The gate of the back fence was open, and Carl led them into the yard. It was prettier than the front yard. Someone had clearly tended it with great love. Two children sat on swings, twisting slowly, making circles in the dirt at their feet, staring at their shoes. Bree had the sudden overwhelming feeling that they were the bereaved. They looked up when the trio came into the yard.

"Hello," Andy said.

"Hey." The little boy looked up, and the look on his face said he was soul-weary of meeting new people. "Food goes inside."

"Uh . . . we don't have food."

"Not them," Carl whispered. "Right back here."

He headed toward a garden with tall hedges at the back of the yard. Over the tops of the hedges, Bree saw a gazebo. Carl took them straight toward it. They stepped around the hedges and into a garden. A man sat alone in the gazebo, his eyes toward the back of the yard.

Carl slowed his steps, but kept heading toward the man. Bree knew what was wrong before she ever looked into his eyes. He was the widower. His wife, the mother of his children, was dead.

The man heard them coming and slowly turned around.

Flash.

She saw him running through the hospital, searching each face and each bed for his wife, screaming out her name, asking if anyone had seen her.

Flash.

She had died in the earthquake, just as they thought. She had been buried in a building just like Bree had. Tears filled her eyes, but she managed to speak.

"Sir, I'm so sorry about your wife."

He looked up at her. "Do I know you?"

"No, but I'm Bree Harris, and this is Andy Hendrix and Carl Dennis. We were all buried in rubble when our building collapsed—" She started to cry and couldn't go on.

He rubbed his eyes. "My wife was pulled out two days ago. She was probably dead the moment the quake happened. Her skull was crushed. She never even knew what hit her." He wiped his eyes and got to his feet. "I'm Lawrence Grisham. How do you know about my wife?"

Andy introduced them. "You're going to think this is weird, but the Lord led us here today. He thought you needed help."

"I do." The man broke down. "I can't do this. I've never been the one people stared at and felt sorry for at a funeral. My poor kids. Those people in my house—I don't know them. They were my wife's friends from church. But I never went with her. Oh, no, I was too busy, too preoccupied. I had better things to do." The words rang with self-hatred.

"And now all these people are here bringing dishes and food and hugs for her parents who are in the house organizing everything. I don't want to talk to those people. All I want is to turn back time just a little bit so I can tell her how much I love her, start going to church with her. That's all she ever really wanted from me, to be a church-going man. But that wasn't what I was, and I wasn't about to change." His face twisted in despair. "What a disappointment I must have been to her."

"You could change now," Andy said. "It's not too late."

"It *is* too late." The man rubbed his hand across his mouth. "She's *gone.*"

"But the children aren't gone." Andy touched his shoulder and gazed in his eyes. "You've still got them. And all the prayers your wife prayed for you have yet to be answered. Do you believe that your wife is in heaven?"

"Absolutely. She's been in love with Jesus ever since I've known her. I fooled her into thinking I was like her before we got married, then slowly but surely I pulled the rug out from under her and showed my true colors. I don't know why she even stayed with me."

"Well, don't you want to see her again?"

"Of course I do, but how can I? I'm not going where she's going. If there's a God, He's probably disgusted with me. In fact, isn't there some Scripture that says He wants to vomit you out of His mouth?"

Andy shook his head. "When He said that, He was talking to Christians who were neither hot nor cold. The truth is, Christ came to save that which was lost, and that's why we're here. We're sort of the same way, seeking and saving that which is lost. And for some reason, God led us to your house today. We didn't know you from Adam, didn't know why people were milling around here, but we saw that there was a need. And the Lord just kind of led us around to the backyard here where we could find you and tell you that He loves you. He hasn't given up on you, Lawrence. You can see your wife again one day, and so can your children, if you can just believe what she believed."

Grisham got up, walked around the gazebo, and turned back toward the house. "I'm a builder, you know. I built half the houses in this neighborhood. I took a lot of pride in my work. I thought I was a great provider for my family. I thought I gave them everything they needed . . . but now I find out just how useless I was."

"Sir, how can you say that? You built a beautiful home here."

"And now my wife is gone! I'm stuck here raising the children, and I don't know what to do. I don't think I've ever been alone with them a day in my life. I love them; don't get me wrong. I just don't know what to do. My wife did it all, and it only now occurs to me how much I needed her. She was everything."

He broke down and slumped down on the bench, dropping his face into his hands. "If only I could be more like her, if I could think the things she thought, feel the feelings she felt. If I could be the kind of person she was, maybe I could raise these kids and do what I need to do by them. But that would be too much of a miracle."

Andy sat beside him. "God's in the business of miracles. Don't you understand that?"

"Then why didn't He save her?"

Bree looked at Andy, wondering how in the world he'd find the wisdom to answer that question.

But Andy wasn't daunted. "He did save her. She was taken to heaven. She's in a safe place. But God's not finished with you, Lawrence. The Lord loves you, and He has you on His mind. He's working in your life whether you can see Him or not."

The man sat there a moment, studying his hands, his forehead pleated as he tried to work it all out. Andy had the grace to let quiet settle over them.

Finally the man got to his feet again and slid his hands into his pockets. "Do you guys have a church, or what?"

"Yes, sir," Bree said, "we do. We go to the same church. It's Brotherhood Community Church over on Chapel Road."

"Well, maybe I need to visit it. I think it would be too painful for my kids to go back to their church, to sit there without their mother. Maybe we need some place new."

"I can understand that," Andy said, "but we're not here to rob churches of their members. We just want to help you."

"Do you have a service tonight?"

"Yes," Bree said, "but are you sure you want to come this soon?"

"Yes, I'm sure." His face took on a determined look. "I made some promises to God while I was sitting at the burial service, and I think it's time I started keeping them. My kids and I will be there tonight. We'll see if God will really give me another chance."

15

CARL'S FEET DIDN'T SEEM TO HAVE A DIRECTION AS they left the Grisham house, so he and the others each decided to go home and rest before church.

Bree's mother was napping when she got home, and her children were still at their friend's.

She went to her room and opened her Bible. She'd never been one to spend a lot of time poring over Scripture, but now she felt it was a missing piece in her life. And it was a piece she needed for the job God had set before her. Even so, she feared it was too late to catch up. The Lord had given her a job to do, but she had flippantly skipped the training.

She opened to Romans and turned a few pages, then her eyes fell to a highlighted passage—Romans 12. Her pastor had preached on this last week, just days before the earthquake. His sermon was about equipping the Body of

Christ and how each believer had different gifts, but all those gifts worked together.

How appropriate! And why was she surprised that the Lord had led her to this today? Smiling, she began to read.

—◇—

The moment Carl was inside his apartment, his feet led him straight to his Bible. It lay open on his bed table, and he picked it up and took it in the living room to the couch. He sat down and turned on the lamp, then opened it to a passage he'd highlighted in yellow. Romans 12.

"I urge you therefore, brethren, by the mercies of God, to present your bodies a living and holy sacrifice, acceptable to God, which is your spiritual service of worship. And do not be conformed to this world, but be transformed by the renewing of your mind . . ."

Carl stopped reading and stared at the page, running those last few words through his mind: *Transformed by the renewing of your mind.*

He thought about those words, over and over, trying to crack the code that had always seemed like gibberish before.

And then he understood. Just because his feet were

running all over the place in his rescue operation for God, it didn't in any way mean he was better than any other Christian. And that meant his mind and heart had some growing to do.

He read on.

. . . "that you may prove what the will of God is, that which is good and acceptable and perfect. For through the grace given to me I say to every man among you not to think more highly of himself than he ought to think; but to think so as to have sound judgment, as God has allotted to each a measure of faith."

Carl got up and paced his apartment, rubbing the back of his neck. He was no super-athlete, running the hundred-yard dash from disaster to broken heart. He was just a short, skinny, bald guy, like he'd always been.

But he was chosen by God, not just to have amazing feet, but for salvation, and eternal life, and a share in Christ's own inheritance. He went back to his Bible and read on.

"For just as we have many members in one body and all the members do not have the same function, so we, who are many, are one body in Christ, and individually members one of another."

He sat back down and stared at a nail hole on his wall.

No doubt about it, the Lord was speaking to him. And with all his heart, he determined that he would listen.

⸺⸺⸺

Andy tried to sleep when he got home, but he kept looking at his Bible, lying open on the desk in the corner of his room. He was dog tired. He had stayed up all night last night, reading Scripture and trying to prepare himself for the situations the Lord would put him in today. But now he felt compelled to read and study more.

He got up and went to his desk, then looked down at the passage on the open page.

And since we have gifts that differ according to the grace given to us, let each exercise them accordingly: if prophecy, according to the proportion of his faith; if service, in his serving; or he who teaches, in his teaching; or he who exhorts, in his exhortation; he who gives, with liberality; he who leads, with diligence; he who shows mercy, with cheerfulness.

Andy frowned. A jolt went through him that the Lord was speaking to him, as clearly as if He had appeared to him. "Why did You show me this, Lord?"

He walked around his small house, processing what he'd read. "We've got these gifts and we've used them together . . . But there are other gifts, and other gifted people . . ."

His voice trailed off, and he picked the Bible up.

"Let love be without hypocrisy. Abhor what is evil; cling to what is good. Be devoted to one another in brotherly love; give preference to one another in honor."

"I will, Lord. No matter what, I will. I understand that the work doesn't stop when we lead people to You. There's more to be done." He swallowed, feeling humbled and small. "Teach me, Lord. I'm listening."

16

B<small>REE'S AFTERNOON OF STUDY LEFT HER FEELING</small> more equipped than ever as she went back to church for the evening service. Carl and Andy waited in the parking lot for her, and she rushed toward them.

"I feel so good! I had a great Bible study this afternoon and I'm ready to go."

"Me too." Andy grinned. "I felt like God was talking right to me."

"I had the same experience," Carl said. "It was awesome."

They started inside. The corridor was crowded with milling people, chattering and laughing before entering the sanctuary. She saw several visitors engaged in conversations with members.

A sickly looking woman with thinning hair and yellow skin met Bree's eyes.

She waited for the flash, but there was none. She glanced at the member who was talking to the woman, and hoped that she was filling the woman's needs.

Bree moved on, following Carl into the crowd, but he walked slowly, with no particular purpose. Andy walked in a brooding silence . . . just as he'd done so often before the quake.

Carl stopped and leaned back against the wall, looking around with a frown on his face. Bree stood there, waiting for him to tell her who to look at, but he was staring at the floor.

She turned and met another woman's eyes.

Nothing.

She looked at a man. A little girl. A teenage boy.

Lord, I don't see.

"Something's happened." Andy's words turned her around, and she frowned up into his somber eyes.

"Yeah, let's find some place to talk. Carl?"

He nodded, but this time he didn't lead them. He followed as Andy led them up the hall.

All the way there, Bree locked into people's gazes, trying to see with her gift, trying to understand their hearts.

But nothing happened.

Finally, they reached the same room they'd gone into the other night, and Carl turned the light on.

"I've lost the gift." They said it simultaneously, then caught their breath.

"You too?" Andy asked. "I thought it was just me."

"I'm walking aimlessly," Carl said. "My feet feel like lead."

Bree shook her head. "And I've met the eyes of a dozen people and haven't had one flash."

Carl sank down and propped his chin on the heels of his hands. "Man, what does *this* mean?"

"Maybe we blew it," Andy said. "Maybe God took our gifts away because we didn't use them well enough."

Bree couldn't believe that was true. "What more could we have done? We went until Carl's urge faded. Then I felt like God was sending us home to rest."

"Then why?" Carl asked. "Why would He give us these precious gifts, then snatch them away?"

Bree shoved her fingers through her hair and tried to think. "You know, it's crazy. When I first got this gift, it scared me to death. Remember when we came in here the other night, and our heads were spinning because we didn't know what was happening? I didn't *want* the gift. But now that I've had it and I've seen its power, I don't want to lose it."

She went to the window and looked out on one of

the parking lots. It was going to be a record crowd for a Sunday night. So many people looking for God.

"Does this mean our work is over?" Carl asked the question on a raspy breath.

Bree turned back around.

"It can't be," Andy said. "A Christian's work is never over. Ours just got started."

"But how can we do it without the gifts?" Carl's question held a note of despair. "We'll go back to being just as useless and ineffective as we were before we got them."

A knock sounded on the door, and Jim, the pastor, stuck his head in. "I saw you guys come in here. Am I interrupting anything?"

Andy got to his feet. "No, come on in, Jim."

"I just wanted to ask you guys a favor. Tonight, I plan to have a testimony time in the service. I'd love to have the three of you talk about your miracle healings and how God's been working in you ever since. Would you mind sharing that with the congregation?"

Bree shot Andy an alarmed look. Carl just kept his eyes on his toes.

"I don't know how helpful we'd be, Jim." Andy cleared his throat. "There must be someone better."

Jim laughed. "Are you kidding? Who? You're the best example I've seen of the body of Christ in action."

Carl looked up. "I could say a few words."

Bree sighed. "Yeah, me too, for what it's worth."

Andy was the last to give in. "All right. I'll think of something to say."

When Jim had left them alone, they all stood there, staring at the door.

"I can't believe I agreed to that," Andy said.

"Me either." Bree crossed her arms. "So I guess we'd better start planning what we're going to say."

Andy sighed. "Well, I guess we tell them about the healing. God didn't take that away from us, did he? My lungs and throat are fine. Carl can still walk. And you can see."

Light began to dawn in Bree's heart. "You know . . . you're right. The healing stands."

Carl got up. "And so does the fruit. God didn't revoke that, did He?"

Bree moved across the room and stood in front of both men. "Are we ungrateful, or what? Here I am feeling sorry for myself because I don't have x-ray vision, and for all intents and purposes, I'm supposed to be blinded beyond help."

"Yeah, and I probably wouldn't have walked for the rest of my life." Carl's eyes grew misty. "I feel like such a heel."

Andy laughed. "No pun intended?"

They all grinned.

"So He gave us the gifts for forty-eight hours," Andy said. "I don't think we need to feel punished because He took them back. We should feel blessed because He let us be a part of such a mighty work. And the truth is, we were all changed. I sure was."

"Yeah, me too." Bree's voice lowered to a soft whisper. "Now that I've had the chance to bear fruit, I don't think I'll ever go back to the way I was before."

"Nope." Carl took both of their hands. "I think maybe we owe God a prayer, a word of thanks, and a petition for His Holy Spirit to help us keep serving Him."

So the three of them prayed.

17

B REE'S CHILDREN MET HER IN THE SANCTUARY AND sat on either side of her in one of the front pews. Andy and Carl sat down the row from her.

As she sat there, warm gratitude washed over her that her life had been spared, that her children were fine, that her eyesight was as good as ever.

But she was different.

Thank You, Lord.

They sang and praised the Lord, then Jim launched into his sermon. Finally, he turned to the trio and asked them to come to the pulpit. As they made their way up, the congregation grew silent.

Andy took the lead. "Two days ago, the three of us were sitting in our office lounge after work, trying to get into a Bible study that was meant to be an outreach to our office. There was only one thing wrong. None of us had bothered to get the word out to the others in the office. So it was just us, and we were pretty pathetic. And then the earthquake came."

Emotion caught his words and twisted his face, and he cleared his throat. "We were buried together, under three floors of rubble. We thought we were going to die, but God had other plans." He broke down and couldn't go on.

Carl stepped up to the microphone. "A fire broke out near Andy, and he had a lot of smoke inhalation, wrecking his vocal cords and his lungs. Bree had something shatter into her eyes, and she was blinded. My legs were crushed into what felt like a zillion pieces." He held out his arms. "We have documented proof. X-rays. Paramedics who treated us. Doctors and nurses. But look at us now."

A slow applause started over the room, and Carl stepped back from the pulpit. Bree took the baton.

"Once we were healed, we felt we needed to give God our best in return, so we've been going out for the past two days, under the power of the Holy Spirit, and He took us to places we ordinarily wouldn't have gone. We met an elderly woman who'd had a stroke and was lying helpless on the floor. We met a woman who'd been abused by a violent husband. We met an alcoholic. We met a man whose pregnant wife had just lost their baby. We met a family who'd just buried their wife and mother."

She looked out over the congregation, and saw Sarah Manning sitting among several members. She was getting more comfortable with the crowds. Dr. John Fryer sat on the second row, his Bible open in his lap. Sam Jones sat near the back, all alone. And Lawrence Grisham sat in the center of the room, his somber children on either side of him.

"I'm different now." Bree struggled to keep her voice steady. "I don't just look past your faces anymore. I see *into* them. I see people who are hurting, people who need help, people who need the Lord. I can't get to them all, and neither can Carl or Andy. We did a lot together, but we need help. We need *your* gifts, all of them."

Andy nodded and stepped up to the mike again. "This morning, the Lord led me to a passage in Romans 12."

Bree caught her breath and gaped at him. That was what she had read!

"I don't believe it," Carl whispered next to her. "I read that same passage."

Andy opened his Bible and started to read. "'For just as we have many members in one body and all the members do not have the same function, so we, who are many, are one body in Christ, and individually members one of another.' I think He wanted us to tell you that we have the gifts we need, as long as we all use them together."

Bree's eyes were full of tears when she moved next to Andy. "We all have gifts," she said. "Every one of us who's in Christ. Supernatural gifts, powered by the Holy Spirit."

Carl moved to stand on the other side of Andy. "There are lots of people out there hurting. Even before the earthquake, they were all around us. We just have to start looking . . . seeing . . . listening . . . going . . . telling . . ."

"Since the earthquake, it's going to be worse," Andy said. "People need the Lord more than ever, and that means they need us. Pastor Jim told us that he wanted us to have a spiritual triage unit here, where the wounded and broken-hearted can come for help and healing. *This* should be the place where people know they'll find Jesus."

The crowd sprang to their feet, applauding the task before them . . . and the One who had equipped them to fulfill it.

18

WHEN THE SERVICE ENDED, THE TRIO FOUND themselves surrounded by members who wanted to help with the spiritual triage, who just needed someone to point them in the right direction.

Bree saw Sam Jones—the man whose wife had lost their baby—through the crowd, quietly waiting to talk to them. Bree excused herself from the conversation she was engaged in and made her way to him.

"Hi, Sam. It's good to see you back tonight."

He nodded. "Yeah. Who would have thought I'd go to church twice in one day?"

"Maybe soon you can bring your wife."

He smiled. "That's what I wanted to talk to you about." He slid his hands into his pockets and swallowed hard. "I was wondering if you guys would mind coming home with me to talk to my wife tonight? She's there with her sister, and she's still really depressed. She needs some hope . . . that maybe she'll see our baby again someday. That she'll get through this. That there's light in the darkness."

"Of course we'll come," Bree said. "Just let me tell the guys."

He blinked back the moisture in his eyes. "Thanks, Bree."

She cut back through the crowd, and as she did so, someone caught her arm. She turned and saw Camille Jackson, a long-time member who'd buried her six-year-old daughter a year ago, after a tragic car accident. "Hi, Camille."

Camille's mouth trembled. "Bree, I know you're busy, but I was so moved by what you said tonight. And I want to help. I've been steeped in grief for the past year, but there were dear church members who helped me through it. And now I'm ready to help somebody else."

Bree's spirit swelled. The Holy Spirit was at it again.

"One of you mentioned that you'd ministered to a man whose pregnant wife had lost her baby. I was thinking that maybe I could help with that."

Bree's heart tugged between laughter and tears. "Oh,

Camille. We're going to talk to her tonight. Would you come with us?"

Her face slowly brightened, and her lips stretched into a smile. "Yes, of course I will. Let me go tell my family."

Bree began to laugh as she watched Camille hurry back through the crowd.

"What's so funny?"

Dabbing her eyes, she turned to find Andy behind her. "The Holy Spirit is still doing supernatural works. He doesn't need us to have superhuman skills." She swallowed and drew in a deep breath. "Andy, we have an appointment tonight with Sam Jones's wife and sister-in-law. And Camille Jackson is coming with us."

———

They found Sharon Jones curled up in a recliner with a blanket over her. Shadows made half circles under her eyes, and grief seemed to have cast a pale pallor over her skin.

She wasn't in the mood for company. Her sister, Shelly, bustled around trying to make the home hospitable as the four of them filed in behind Sam and squeezed together on the couch.

Sam knelt next to her. "Honey, I know you don't feel

like talking, but I'm worried about you, and I think these people can help."

Andy leaned forward and cleared his throat. He had rehearsed his speech all the way over, but as he opened his lips to speak, Camille jumped in.

"Sharon, I lost my little girl a year ago. I think I know something of what you're going through."

Sharon straightened instantly, and that glazed look in her sad eyes faded. Her eyes locked onto Camille's face. "You did? How old was she?"

"She was six. She was hit by a car when she ran out of the yard to chase a ball." Camille had trouble getting the words out, and the pain on her face reflected that on Sharon's.

Sharon nodded. "People think that since my baby hadn't been born, since I hadn't held him alive in my arms, hadn't heard his voice, hadn't lived with him at home, that it wasn't like losing a real child."

"I don't think that," Camille whispered. "He was your baby, and you had your heart invested in him. You felt every kick, every movement. You heard his heart beating at every doctor visit."

Sharon started to cry. "I saw him sucking his thumb on the ultrasound."

Camille wiped her own tears. "I know. He was your son, and you're going to hurt for a long time."

Sharon brought the blanket up to cover her face as she wilted. Camille got up and knelt beside Sharon's chair, stroking her hair. "Are you going to have a funeral for your baby?"

Sharon sucked in a sob and looked at her husband. "My mother thinks it's a bad idea. That it would be too painful. That it would drag things out. But I want to have one. I want to honor his little life. I want to have a place I can go . . ."

"You could still have one," Camille said. "I think it would be nice. I think it would help you a lot. I'll help you plan it if you want."

Andy looked at Bree and Carl, and Bree understood his silent message: They weren't really needed here. There was little they could add. Camille was the one Sharon needed now.

When the time was right, they left Camille talking to Sharon, and Sam walked them to the door. "I don't know how to thank you. She's been closed up ever since it happened. I didn't even know she wanted a funeral. For a stranger to come here and love her like that, to bond with her in such a way . . . I just don't know what to think."

"Think the obvious," Andy said. "Think that the Lord loves you and Sharon so much that He sent the only person in our church who knew exactly what to say."

As they got back into the car, all three of them still struggled with the emotion constricting their throats. Finally, Andy managed to speak.

"You know, I went there with every intention of sharing the plan of salvation with her. Of closing the deal. Helping them pray the prayer. But the Holy Spirit taught me something I didn't expect."

"Me too," Bree said. "He taught us that we have to love first. That's what hurting people respond to."

Carl nodded. "It doesn't take fancy-shmancy sales tactics for people to come to Christ. They'll be drawn to Him automatically if we just love them. Who isn't drawn by love?"

19

SEVERAL OF THE CHURCH MEMBERS HAD EXPRESSED a desire to help May by cleaning up her house, stocking her cabinets, cooking some meals, and doing repairs on her house, so the trio headed to the hospital to ask her for the key. They were still pensive and quiet as they rode the elevator to her floor.

May's door was pulled almost shut, so Bree raised her hand to knock. But then she heard voices in the room and pushed the door slightly open to see if she was interrupting anything.

Dr. John Fryer sat next to May's bed, a Bible in his lap, reading from the book of Matthew. Sarah sat on the other side of the bed, holding the old lady's hand, and soaking in every word.

Bree knocked.

"Come in, come in!" May grinned at the trio. "All my new friends. The Lord is so good."

The sight of three to whom they'd ministered, ministering now to each other, filled Bree with such poignant feelings that she didn't trust her voice. "How are you, May?"

May reached up to hug her. "I'm wonderful. How could I not be?"

Andy and Carl hugged her too. "We don't want to interrupt this Bible study," Andy said. "But May, some of the church members wanted to bring food to your house and do some cleaning and repair work. We wanted to get your permission."

"Well, of course. Those dear people. They must have known I'd be going home tomorrow."

"Tomorrow?" Bree looked at Dr. John.

"I'm releasing her tomorrow, since I know that Sarah's going to be there to help her at home. She'll have to come back every day for physical therapy, but Sarah has committed to getting her here."

Sarah smiled. Her countenance was so different than what they'd seen in her just days earlier. "I'll take real good care of her."

"I know you will," Bree said.

Carl clapped his hands. "Well, that means that the food and help is coming in the nick of time. Would you give us a key so we could let them in tonight? Some of the members are all set to get busy."

May smiled over at Sarah. "I gave my key to Sarah, but she could go with you and let you in. Sarah, you run along with them, honey, and you supervise. One of us needs to be there to thank those darling folks."

Sarah left with them, her still-bruised face glowing. They drove over to May's house and saw that several cars already waited in front of her yard. Sarah let them in and accepted a hug from each person as they bustled in, joy and peace pulsating from them as they set about to work for the Lord by loving Sarah and May.

Bree, Carl, and Andy worked until after eleven that night. They were the last to leave, but as they looked around at the house that had been so dusty and drab before the church members had cleaned it up, they knew it would provide a sweet welcome home to May tomorrow. Sarah bustled around as if she'd already made herself at home, excited that she could now begin to pass the love she'd found on to someone else.

Bree was sure the guys were as tired as she by the time they left the house. As they got into the car, they saw headlights approaching them. The car slowed down next to theirs, and Andy looked in the window.

Lawrence Grisham, the man who'd buried his wife earlier that day, sat behind the wheel. "I was hoping I'd catch you. After church tonight, I heard about the lady who lives here. Some of the members were making plans to help her. I would have come sooner, but it took me a long time to get the kids to bed tonight. Their grandparents are at the house now, so I wanted to run over and offer some help."

Bree shot Carl an amazed look.

"That's really great of you," Andy said. "But we're about finished here. We stocked the kitchen, and several of the ladies brought casseroles and stuff. And we gave the house a real thorough cleaning."

Lawrence nodded. "Well, I thought of something I could do. I'm a builder, you know. I thought I'd come over here with my crew tomorrow and make the house wheelchair accessible. I heard the woman's paralyzed on one side, so she'll be in a wheelchair for a while."

Andy stood up straight and looked back at the two of them. Bree and Carl both began to cry.

Lawrence seemed puzzled by their reaction, so he shifted his car into park and got out, peering at them over the hood. "Did I say something wrong?"

Bree shook her head. "No, not at all." She went around

the car and hugged the man. "I'm just so amazed at the way God works."

She felt his body shake as he hugged her back.

"I was just thinking the same thing," he whispered.

20

CARL WAS QUIET AS HE PULLED INTO BREE'S driveway, and Andy leaned up on the seat and patted her shoulder.

"It's been fun, guys," Bree said. "I'll never forget the things we've done these last few days."

"I know," Andy said. "I'll be changed forever."

Carl set his wrist on the steering wheel and looked at a spot on his windshield. "I miss my gift, though. I felt so anointed there for a while. I was so full of purpose."

Andy sighed. "We still have purpose, Carl. And we *are* anointed."

"We are," Bree agreed. "We're chosen, and God has given us work to do. It was really great having God work through us like that. But you know something? I've felt God working through us tonight too, even since our gifts went away. He did things just as mighty and amazing as

He did when I could see with His eyes, or when Carl walked with His feet, or when Andy spoke with His tongue."

Andy started to laugh softly. "And the best part was seeing Him work like that in the rest of our church. Everyone having a purpose. Every purpose working together."

"And the fruit bearing fruit."

Bree shifted on the seat so that she could look Andy fully in the face. "We can't go back to the way we were before. I don't ever want to ignore all those needy people around me again. I don't want to be useless anymore."

"Me, either," Carl said. "I've devoted my feet to the Lord from this point on. I'm going where I'm told. Like Isaiah 52:7 says, 'How lovely on the mountains are the feet of him who brings good news, who announces peace and brings good news of happiness, who announces salvation, and says to Zion, "Your God reigns!"'"

Bree squeezed Carl's arm. "I'm going to devote my feet to Him too. And I'm going to try to keep seeing with His eyes."

"'Blessed are the eyes which see,'" Andy said. "Luke 10:23. You know what I'm going to do? I'm going to keep studying my Bible, so I can be ready in season and out of season. So that I can know God's truths well enough to speak it boldly."

"Let's all vow to do that," Bree said.

"From now on," Carl agreed, "let's be ready to speak the praises of God."

Andy nodded. "Just like Zacharias did in Luke 1:64."

"We may have lost our gifts," Bree said. "But we're still so gifted because of Christ and all He's given us. And when we go back to work and we start trying to invite people to our Bible study again, I think it'll be different this time. This time, we'll be using the power we have in the Holy Spirit. Loving them, filling their needs, attracting them to what we are in Christ." She grinned. "This time we won't leave it all up to e-mails and brochures."

"I'm with you." Carl reached out to take her hand. "We're a team."

Andy put his hand over both of theirs. "All for One, and One for All. That's God's plan for His Body."

"What a plan it is," Bree whispered. "What an awesome, amazing plan."

Study Guide Questions

1. Merriam Webster's Dictionary defines "ministry" as "a person or thing through which something is accomplished." Applying that definition to the Christian faith, I would add that Christian ministry is "a person or thing through which something is accomplished to further Christ's kingdom." What have you done lately to further the kingdom of Christ?

2. In your church, are there two groups—those who serve and those being served? Which group are you in?

3. What are some excuses people use for not getting involved in ministry?

4. Some believe the paid ministers in your church are the ones who should do all the work in furthering the Kingdom. Read Ephesians 4:11–12. What does Paul say the ministerial staff are supposed to do? Who is supposed to do the actual "work of service"?

5. List the attributes of those in your church who seem to do everything. For instance, are they compassionate? Are they merciful? Do they have special skills? What makes them better suited for ministry than others? Are they really better suited, or are they just more willing?

6. Read Romans 12, then list the gifts in this passage. Do your gifts fit into any of these categories?

7. What crises or trials in your life might have prepared you for helping others?

8. What would a "spiritual triage" look like in your church?

9. Are there examples in your church, or in your area of ministry, where you've seen your fruit bearing fruit?

10. What attributes in your personality or skill sets could help further the kingdom of Christ?

11. At the end of your life, what would you like to have accomplished? Write an obituary of your life, the way you'd like for it to read. Then ask God to help you live that kind of life.

More from TERRI BLACKSTOCK

The Gifted Sophomores

After being pulled from the rubble of an earthquake, three socially mismatched teens are given supernatural gifts that make them an evangelism task force that cannot be stopped. But will their passion and power continue if their gifts fade?

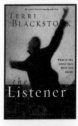

The Listener

For two weeks, Sam Bennett is given an extraordinary gift: hearing as God hears. Frightened at first, he begins to use his gifts to touch others and radically transform his own life.

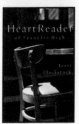

The Heart Reader of Franklin High

What if you could hear as God hears? Jake Sheffield can. He can hear the deepest needs of people around him, although they aren't saying anything. Is Jake going crazy, or is God about to do something amazing?

Covenant Child

Twins Kara and Lizzie grew up in squalor, never guessing the riches held in trust for them or the love that lived to call them home. Now they must choose between the familiar and the extraordinary.

Terri Blackstock

A Division of Thomas Nelson Publishers